# 52 For 52

*A Collection*

---

Adam Drake

This is a work of fiction. Names, characters, places, and incidents either are the product of the author's imagination or are used fictitiously. Any resemblance to actual persons, living or dead, events, or locales is entirely coincidental.



Published in the United States by Smokestack Entertainment Publishing.

SMOKESTACK ENTERTAINMENT PUBLISHING and its logo are trademarks of Smokestack Entertainment, LLC.

Library of Congress Cataloging-in-Publication data is available upon request.

ISBN 9780578442907

*For Lindsey*

Contents

---

*A Note*

---

*I spend the majority of my days writing scripts, social posts, billboards, and presentations for clients, and my desire to write my own stories at home became more of a hassle rather than a pleasure. And so, I devised a challenge for myself: write one story a week for an entire year. No matter where the story was at the end of the week, I had to publish it. It seemed daunting during the first few weeks, but as I slid into December, I was saddened at the thought that this little project was coming to an end. Some of these stories need a lot of work, or fall apart under intense scrutiny. Others are deeply personal and probably act more as therapy than short stories. And finally, there are a few in here that are genuinely good. It's those stories that make me want to keep going, to keep writing, to work on something bigger.*

*Thanks for indulging me. Thanks for taking the journey. And above all else, thanks for reading.*

*-Adam*

# 52 Storeys

## *Week One*

She'd never claim to be a numbers person. Math wasn't her strong suit. But despite that, she knew she had more than anyone else. More followers. More fame. More importance. And from Madison's lofty perch, she knew those numbers were about to increase ten-fold.

This all started more than 25 years ago, back when Madison Light was known by her birth name, "Melissa Lowenstein." She'd sung a note-perfect rendition of "Part of Your World" from *The Little Mermaid* to Suzie whatever-her-name-was during recess. Suzie responded with praise, and from that day on, Madison was addicted. Her parents enrolled her in singing lessons, acting classes, and dance schools. Next came the parts in school plays: Ophelia, Annie, and Maria.

Ovations. Flowers. Clippings in the town newspaper complimenting the "choices" she took in each role. This was followed closely by an appearance in a local television commercial for *Manny's Muffler Shop* in which she'd absolutely crushed the role of "Teenage Girl #2." Like a call to prayer, everyone in the Lowenstein household had to stop what they were doing and gawk in silence whenever the commercial came on.

More auditions. More headshots. A name change. A boob job. And suddenly, Madison Light was about to conquer the world. She'd managed to score a starring role in a Saturday morning kid's show, which led to a country-wide concert tour. Then an international tour. This, of course, was followed by a conveniently crafted romance with another rising star - whom she'd only meet up with for photo opportunities while leaving fashionable restaurants.

Paparazzi chased her car. Articles were written about her diet tips. Facebook pages were created to worship her. She had to install cameras and a 24-hour security detail at her home in Montecito to keep out stalkers. She made a ton of money, but never paid for anything.

Every single morning, before she put her blue-eyed contacts in, before she had a sip of espresso from her specifically-designed in-wall *Miele* machine, she'd grab her phone and look at her number of followers. For a while, she'd flip out if the number dropped between days. Then, she'd flip out if the number of new daily followers was below her average. Now, calls would be made to publicists, managers, and agents if - God forbid - Selena Gomez or Taylor Swift's follower numbers got close to hers.

---

She'd arrived in New York a week ago when she'd finished publicity for her latest romantic comedy, and early estimates were predicting it would open at number one. But despite all this success, something was nagging her. Something that she couldn't shake. This horrible notion that, when all was said and done, she had nowhere to go. She had nothing left to conquer. Politics? No, they take too much of a look into your private life. Sports? No, too risky. She didn't want to end up on some trashy website with a black eye because a basketball hit her in the face.

It took a few days of serious consideration before she came to a realization. A solution. The next step in her career would be her greatest. It would immortalize her. They'd speak of her forever. She'd join the likes of Marilyn Monroe, Princess Di, and, if she was going to be honest, Jesus Christ.

She had to die.

The theme song to *Fame* said it best, "I want to live forever." And goddamn it, she was going to live forever, even if it killed her. Plus, her death just before the opening of her movie would absolutely guarantee it would open at number one. The movie studio should build her a statue.

---

She'd counted each of the 52 floors up to the roof as the elevator bell ticked them off. Each ring brought her closer to legend. She'd chosen this particular building for several reasons:

1. It wasn't on a crowded street, so the risk of accidentally killing someone - beside herself - on her way down was minimal.
2. The sidewalk was recently redone, so the inevitable pictures of her demise would look clean and sophisticated without the decades-old gum that plagues most Manhattan sidewalks.
3. You couldn't beat the view.

She'd determined that flinging herself off the top of a building was the most dramatic way to go. Overdoses were so typical and quickly going out of fashion. Wrist cutting was almost Elizabethan. Drowning too uncomfortable. And hanging was too barbaric. Suicide by jumping just felt right. After all, she'd always wanted to go skydiving.

Then, of course, there was the topic of a suicide note. She'd gone back and forth on it, but ultimately decided not to leave one. Less is more, right?

Leave them guessing. She'd probably get an extra few days of news coverage out of it. First, of course, they'd look for one. Then they'd spend a considerable amount of time asking why; talking to her third tier "friends" about how they'd seen signs all along. But ultimately, it would be inconclusive and this unknowingness would help fuel her legend.

Madison sat on the side of the building with her feet dangling over the edge, her green dress (specifically chosen because it went so well with blood red) flapped in the updrafts. She stared out over the city and the millions of people pulsing around. She wondered how long it would take for the news agencies to pick up word of her death. How many phones would vibrate in unison as the words "Madison Light has died" crossed their screens. She wished she could be around to see it.

52 storeys on top of the world with an immeasurable audience in front of her, and a feeling crept over her - she'd never felt so alone. Madison took out her phone, opened her Instagram app and took a look at how many followers she had and smiled. She clutched the phone, looked over the abyss, and let go.

# Practice, Practice, Practice

## *Week Two*

Mitch has the midwestern good looks and smooth charm that give him the uncanny ability to convince people to do anything. He had all the charisma of a cult leader and the positive vibes of a motivational speaker. So when he asked me to help him write the music to a song he'd written, and then perform it on the vaunted stage of Carnegie Hall, I gave him the following responses in succession:

"I'm happy to write it. I just don't want to perform it."

"I'm still on board to help write it. But maybe I can record it and you can sing to it."

"What if I taught someone how to play it?"

And finally, "Fine! But I'll probably shit my pants on stage."

A doctor was still six years away from diagnosing me with a severe anxiety disorder, and so my excuses of "I really don't like to perform in front of people," had no clinical basis. Which is why, in the early summer of 2005, I found myself dressed in a tuxedo backstage at one of the most famous music halls in the world about to perform a song on the piano in front of friends, family, co-workers and strangers.

Oh, and I should mention that I don't know how to play the piano.

---

Perhaps understanding my limited musical knowledge, Mitch brought our co-worker and talented guitarist, Tom, on board. Mitch had written the lyrics to "*Mi Amor Estranada*" before he even mentioned this gig to me. So we had some sort of base to start from when we began writing the music in February. That gave us about four months to create, practice, and master our song for the "A Gift of Life" concert. It also gave me about four months to figure out a way to get out of this.

The event itself was created by a New York voice teacher and former opera singer - a way to showcase her students' talents while donating proceeds from the concert to the American Red Cross. My feeling was this: if I accidentally broke all of my fingers in a printing press just before our song, all of those who bought tickets would still get to see a fantastic concert while donating money to a worthy cause. Everyone wins - except for me - who'd have learn to live with hooks for hands. It'd be worth it.

We rehearsed every chance we could. We rented rehearsal space in music studios throughout the city. We practiced at Mitch's apartment (the only one of us who had an apartment big enough to accommodate three people and a piano). Mitch even managed to get us into Carnegie Hall during an off day so we could rehearse on stage and get a feel for the acoustics.

This "soft opening" at Carnegie Hall ended up being the first time all of us had performed in front of an audience that didn't consist of our girlfriends, so my nerves took over. While pulling out the piano bench, I slammed my enormous head into the keys and managed to play a chord with my forehead not unlike the chord at the end of *A Day in the Life*. This, of course, drew strange looks from the stage manager, and I realized I had one more thing to worry about on the night of our performance.

---

While all of this was happening, I'd begun dating someone. Aly was supportive, gave me notes on small things I could do to help improve the performance, and was genuinely excited to see her boyfriend perform on stage at Carnegie Hall. Because our relationship was so new, I'd yet to tell her about my crippling anxiety. I'm sure she saw inklings of it, such as my hatred of crowded rooms, the way I'd sweat when more than one person paid attention to me at a time, and how I'd started walking a few miles across town to work in order to avoid the subway.

What's more, Aly hadn't met my parents yet. They were coming in from out of town to see me play (though my mom said, "Wait, you can play the piano?"), and they'd meet her for the first time in the lobby before the show. They would be entering dark territory, and I (wrongly) assumed they'd spend the time talking about all the mental issues I had and/or my sex life.

---

Finally, after months of rehearsing and waiting, the day of dread had arrived.

All three of us worked a few short blocks away from Carnegie Hall, so, in an effort to blow off pre-show jitters, we made the wise decision to run to the concert. Three grown men, in tuxedos, running at full-tilt through midtown Manhattan at rush hour, in the high humidity of a June afternoon. So yes, I burned off nervous energy, but now my hands were sweaty, which meant my fingers were sweaty, which meant they'd easily slip off the keys when I played. I grabbed every piece of tissue I could shoved them into my pockets, and held my hands in there until our performance in a bad attempt to absorb the sweat.

I looked at Mitch and blamed him - silently - for everything that was currently wrong in my life. I was about to embarrass myself in front of some of the best musicians in New York City, my friends would shake their heads in horror as I defecated all over the piano bench, and my new girlfriend would discover my parents kept me in the Special Ed class until high school because I'd failed to understand tangrams and proper vowel pronunciation. All that I'd worked for throughout my entire life was about to come crashing down in a heap of sweat, blood, and piano wires.

The order of the program was pasted outside the stage door. We were fourth, preceded by several singers and one piano soloist. The piano soloist was Peng Peng, a 12 year old slightly rotund Asian boy who'd played the piano in his mother's womb. His name, a repeated monosyllabic shout out to the instrument he'd hold so dear throughout his life, appeared just as "Cher" or "Madonna" or "Liberace" would in the program. There was no need to add to this kid's name; doing so would take away from what really mattered - his talent. Peng Peng, with his intimidating skill, would be opening the concert.

We had a television in our dressing room which had a closed circuit feed to the stage. We could see and hear each performance live. After a quick introduction by the organizer, Peng Peng was brought on stage to play his song. The kid was good. So good, that as his fingers worked their way over the keys, I swore I saw him lean in close and play part of the song with his tongue. Halfway through the song, I'd had enough and turned off the television. I was sure I'd be the biggest disappointment of the night.

I remember the stage manager calling us to the stage. Walking out, I caught sight of my girlfriend, and thought she looked great in that dress. I didn't want it to be the one she wore when she called me a failure and broke up with me, in front of my parents, later that night. I also remember my hand shaking over the first chord and it coming down correctly.

That's it. The song finished, people clapped, and we walked off the stage.

No shitting of the pants. No passing out. No cracking my over-size head on the horribly expensive and definitely above my pay grade/ability piano keys.

We'd made it. We'd played Carnegie Hall - to what level of success was to be determined. We were happy we made it and walked around the block, slapping each other on the backs, overjoyed that it went well.

The concert ended and we made our way out into the audience. After formally introducing my girlfriend to my parents, a measure met with the ominous "oh, we've already met", I asked what they thought. My mom said, "We'll tell you later." This, in my book, meant that we were horrible. I never expected us to be mind-blowing, but upon reflection, I thought the performance was adequate if not reasonably good. But was it so bad that my parents couldn't find the right words to explain it? They needed time to properly craft their words? Had I missed something?

And I had. I'd missed a lot actually. Because I'd turned the closed circuit television off, we didn't see the other performances, save for Peng Peng's epic concoction of music and skill. According to those who witnessed it, and unfortunately paid good money to witness it, the other performances were absolutely awful. My mother claims to have thought about painful childhood memories to keep from laughing. Aly, seated a row in front of my parents, stifled her laughter so much that she transferred it through forced coughing. At dinner afterward, they spoke animatedly about the horrors they'd just witnessed. One particular performer was so awful that he is, to this day, imitated at family functions, and used as a measure of awful. What's more, everyone praised our performance and said, without question, it was one of the best of the night.

---

I've never returned to the stage at Carnegie Hall. Mitch, Tom, and I played together a few times, but never in front of a crowd and mostly for our own enjoyment. I vaguely remember the chords and arpeggios to *"Mi Amor Estranada"* but haven't played them on a piano in over ten years. And while my anxiety is well taken care of now, I have absolutely zero desire to ever perform in front of people again.

The old adage goes, "the way to get to Carnegie Hall is through practice, practice practice." But that isn't entirely true. Sometimes, all it takes is not shitting yourself while everyone you know is watching.

## Thank You, Lord, For Sending Me The F Train

*Week Three*

McIntyre didn't take the subway home. Like all the other higher ups, he took one of the black cars that waited outside the building like a herd of idling buffalo. While they whisked the important people to exotic locations like Scarsdale or Darien, Palmer had to take the F train - God's rattling underground dumpster - home to a studio apartment in an unnamed corner of Brooklyn.

He was well positioned for the extraordinary. Exceptional schooling. Wonderful grades. A name-brand business school. But once Palmer got into the real world, he found the crushing reality that he was, just like almost everyone else, extra ordinary. And so, he stood in the vestibule of the F train, back turned to the huddled masses in the car, watching his disgruntled reflection melt through the windows of the train doors.

As the train left the 2nd Avenue Station, a homeless man walked through spouting the same monologue Palmer had heard time and again from any number of different basement people.

"Sorry to interrupt..."

"My family is struggling..."

"God bless..."

As he got closer, Palmer subconsciously curled closer to the door, while holding his breath. As if the stench of the man would somehow seep into his lungs and cause communicable poverty. McIntyre was probably in

Riverdale by now, sipping on whatever foreign wine his driver kept stocked in the back of the car.

The train came to a halt, sending Palmer bouncing into the door. The homeless man, trying to gain purchase, grabbed Palmer's arm to steady himself. Palmer glared and the man looked up at him with a pale face filled with concern and fright.

Under his breath and shaking, he said, "Beware the Grundleboch."

Palmer shook his arm loose, confused and annoyed, and turned back to the window, his coat sleeve now lousy with hobo sludge. He turned the phrase quickly over in his mind, but realized it to be the ravings of a drunk and weathered mind.

The homeless man shuffled down the car and the train shifted, connecting with the third rail which sent a spark of blue light illuminating the tunnel. In that flash, Palmer noticed that the tunnel wall in front of him next to the train had crumbled away revealing a dark void beyond. He leaned closer to get a better look.

The New York City underground had been ripped up, drilled through, and built upon so many times, that there were literal caverns and unmapped labyrinths below the city. Hallways spun into themselves. Chasms dropped hundreds of feet toward the bedrock below. And foundations from buildings long forgotten created chambers where all manner of things could hide. The city below was just as expansive as the city above.

Palmer had taken the F train countless times, but he'd never noticed the opening in the tunnel wall between 2nd Avenue and Delancey Street before.

A second, brighter, flash from the third rail lit the space again, and this time Palmer saw something far in the distance. What looked like a man, running toward him, his clothing torn and flowing like ribbons behind him.

But just as suddenly as the light came, it dissipated into nothing. Just darkness. Palmer looked over his fellow passengers to see if anyone saw what he'd just seen. Nothing. Everyone had their faces in the phones, books, and magazines.

The train tilted again, followed by another flash. This time, there was no mistaking the man running toward the train, but closer now. Behind him, giving chase was something. Something not human. Palmer struggled to make out this creature in the fleeting burst of light, all he could see were horns, and fur, and eyes that seemed to hold the light for a few seconds after the flash.

"Jesus Christ..." Palmer stammered.

Instinctively, Palmer stepped back from the door. And the same curious force that pushed him away drove him closer. He leaned again into the darkness, hoping to see what this - thing - was.

A final connection with the third rail sent sparks and light cascading through the tunnel and down into the abyss. This time, the picture was too clear. The man was only a dozen feet in front of Palmer, his hand outstretched, pleading for someone to save him from his pursuer. Behind him, the beast's mouth dripped with saliva and his great meaty arms swung above his horned head.

And then blackness. Blackness followed by the sound of heavy liquid hitting the side of the train. Palmer's head kicked back at the sound of the wet thud. He reached down and through his jacket making sure whatever it was he'd heard and seen hadn't injured him. He wiped sweat off his brow, took his first breath in what seemed like minutes, and looked around the car once more. No one had seen a thing. Palmer thought you could bring the reanimated corpse of Don Knotts into the New York Subway System and no one would bat an eye.

Palmer took one more look out the window, but saw nothing but his own reflection. He needed sleep. Or caffeine. Or a new job.

The train began moving once again, and Palmer turned his back to the window. He may have hallucinated it all, but he sure as shit didn't feel like staring out the windows anymore.

Sound travels slower in stressful situations. It takes more time for each synapse to ignite as tones make their way through a brain that's under duress. Such was the case as the train moved into the lights of the Delancey Street Station and Palmer heard a scream that appeared to be miles away.

But he saw the woman across from him with her mouth open, and then the noise fully hit him. Everyone in the train stared and pointed in his direction. Parents were shielding their children's eyes. People on the platform looked on in horror. Slowly, he turned around, and saw the unmistakable sight of translucent blood mixed with sinewy chunks of skin pouring slowly down the outside of the subway window lit so splendidly by the lights of the Delancey Street Subway Station.

## Ripped for the Headlines

*Week Four*

He turned off the television and, with a an exasperated heave, turned his chair away from his desk. Through the murk of on-coming dusk and past the leaf-less trees, he could just make out the thick obelisk of the Washington Monument. Erected in honor of a man who made this country great, it always gave him pleasure to hold the memorial in his mind. He thought about the huge and amazing monuments that would soon be built in his honor.

The knock on the door was unexpected, and it pulled President Trump out of his daydream. His executive assistant, Madeleine Westerhout, stood in the doorway.

"Sir," she said, "Vice President Pence is here to see you."

"Right. Give me one minute," he replied out of his pursed lips.

She closed the door, and Trump quickly, well, quickly for a man of his girth, shot up from his desk. He adjusted the lights so that they dimmed a bit. He grabbed some unread documents labeled "Important" and strew them about his desk. He wouldn't want Pence to think he wasn't working. Finally, after his tiny hands struggled for purchase on the handle of his desk drawer, he pulled out some sweet mint gum, placed it in his mouth, and rolled the ball around with his tongue.

"Please send the Vice President in," Trump buzzed.

The door opened, and in walked Mike Pence. Trump noticed how his crisp navy-blue suit hugged this round shoulders. And how his white hair looked so much like the snow-frosted peaks that dotted the background of the Trump International Hotel & Tower™ in Vancouver.

"Mike, so good to see you," he shyly stammered out.

"You too, Mr. President," replied a stern Pence.

"Please, have a seat."

The two sat across from each other on couches, Trump's legs spread wide to give him a sense of power and alpha sexuality while also giving his thighs a brief chance not to rub against each other.

"Mr. Presi-"

"Please Mike, we're friends, I've asked you to call me Donald J. Trump."

"Right, Donald J. Trump, I have some documents that I need to review with you regarding reducing tariffs on several West African nations."

Trump looked around much like one would before telling a sexist or racist joke. With a whisper, he said, "You mean countries with ... *those* people?"

"Unfortunately, yes."

Trump let out a sigh, "Fine, let me see them."

Trump and Pence stood up at the same time, and as Pence passed the folio to Trump, their hands grazed each other. The world stopped and they both locked eyes. This touch was something they'd both been wanting for so long.

Trump thought about how smooth Pence's hand felt, not unlike the soft golf towels available at the Trump Turnberry™ in Scotland.

The documents fell to the ground and they held each other's heads in their hands. Pence grabbed the crucifix necklace from around his neck and pulled it off.

"I won't be needing this tonight," he said, tossing the cross away into the plush carpet of the office.

Sensing that things were moving quickly, Trump took off his "Make America Great Again" cap and quickly ran his hand through the straw-like bramble of his hair. He took off his tie and began unbuttoning his shirt.

"Donald J. Trump, " Pence whispered with warm breath, "Let me do it."

Pence's fingers moved quickly, unbuttoning Trump's shirt. He then reached around Trump's back and unbuttoned the girdle; releasing the gelatinous masses of fat that cascaded down Trump's sides and stomach.

For the first time, Pence got a full view of the most powerful man in the world, and saw that his spray tan had missed the folds of his stomach, striping his body like a tiger.

"Pence, there's something you should know before this goes any further."

"It's okay sir, you can tell me anything. I won't mind whatever it is."

"I... uh..."

"What is it?" Pence pleaded.

"You'll have to see for yourself." And with that, Trump lifted up his mighty panniculus, and pulled out what appeared to be a five day-old roast beef sandwich.

"Sir?" Pence asked, confused.

"Yes Pence, I store food in the various folds of my body. I-"

Pence held his finger up to Trump's mouth, demanding he no longer speak. He then reached down and took a bite out of the wet sandwich. Stifling a gag, he smiled at the President.

Trump's hand caressed Pence's face. A light five o'clock shadow had formed on his face, and the rough dots of hair were just like the sandy beach of the Trump Ocean Club™ in Panama. God he wanted his swollen tongue to dart over every inch of the Indiana-native's face.

Trump quickly grabbed his office phone and dialed Westerhout.

"Madeline, hold my calls," he punctuated into the mouth piece, "I'm about to debrief the Vice President."

Once the phone slammed down, their bodies became an instant tangle of old-man skin. Tongues touched tongues, hands groped bodies, and fingers explored the deep moist caverns of Trump's torso.

Trump took a moment to look at his Vice President. He noticed how Pence's abs looked pale and chiseled, which took him immediately to the pale and chiseled toilets of the Trump International Hotel™ in Las Vegas.

As the two bodies became one, Trump could feel the oval office spinning. He'd wanted this for so long, and it's so rare that actuality beats expectation. Still, as with the other five times he'd experienced sexual intimacy, he knew there was only one way he could climax.

Grabbing the long slender black remote of his office television, he pressed the "power" button. On the screen flashed the beautifully crafted face of Steve Doocy. Trump had a back catalog of *Fox & Friends* queued on his DVR should just such an occasion arise. Seeing Doocy, Trump finally exploded with passion. A tear ran down Vice President Pence's face.

They held each other on the couch for a few more minutes. Doocy's punctuation seemed to match the cadence of their heavy breathing. Stroking his white hair, Trump looked down at Pence and said, "This has been more thrilling than the day I closed on Trump Vineyard Estates™ in Charlottesville."

# Coxsackie

*Week Five*

Leave it to a man who creates running routes and flies his drone in the shapes of penises to get some disease called "Coxsackie."

But wait, Adam, isn't Coxsackie a virus that only children get? Yeah, that's what I thought, too. In fact, when I brought my daughter to the pediatrician to get HER diagnosed with Coxsackie, Dr. "I Must Have Skipped Virology Day in Med School" said there was "no way" I would get it. She said, "Adults don't get Coxsackie." In other words, I could take my diseased daughter back home, and play with her to my heart's content because my white blood cells have me covered.

Well, my white blood cells can eat a bag of micropenises.

Coxsackie - also known as hand, foot, and mouth disease, but let's be honest here - "coxsackie" is a far more funny term - is a virus that children between the ages of birth and three get. And wouldn't you know it, my 15 month old daughter got it. Great. She *should* get it. She's the target demographic for it. She's literally an ideal consumer of the Coxsackie virus. But for an adult of 38 - I shouldn't even be on the same page as the Venn Diagram of "people who will get Coxsackie."

So, let's talk about how you get Coxsackie, because it's fucking disgusting. At some point last week, a fleck of fecal dust jumped out of my daughter's asshole, and ninja-kicked its way onto my tongue. Yep, I basically and unintentionally ate a piece of my daughter's shit which carried the virus. It then spread like bad acid at a hippy concert through my body.

Then, this goddamn disease starts firing warning shots at me. Sore throat. Fever. A blister on my lip that looks like herpes. (It's not herpes) It's when red dots start showing up *all over my body* that I realize something isn't right. When Malin got Coxsackie, she got a few blisters on her face, hands, and legs. Gross, but manageable. After all, the disease is also known as "Hand, Food, and Mouth Disease" so it's staying true to its name.

But then, for the love of fuck, it decided to go rogue. I've got blisters on my hands, feet, and face. I've got them in my mouth, on my tongue, and soft palate. They're on my ear lobes. I have them on my back and wrist. I have them in my nostrils. I have them *underneath* my fingernails.

What. The. Absolute. Fuck.

Because they're on my feet, each step I take feels like I'm walking on glass. Because my fingers are covered, I hurts too much to put my socks on. In fact, my eyes watered when I pressed the button to release the seatbelt in my car yesterday.

And you'd think this would be enough. How much more can a man take. Well, I've got news for you. These red blisters all over my body? Yeah, the only way they go away is by pussing and scabbing over. So I'm about a day away from having thousands of weeping sores all over my body which will make me look like a nacho cheese fountain at a shitty wedding.

At this point, it's time for drastic actions. I love my daughter. I'm crazy about her. She's kind, she's smart, and she's beautiful. But she is more diseased than my computer after I "discovered" that Russian monkey porn site. So, for my own health, it's time to let her go. The keys are in the ignition. No questions asked. She's all yours.

## The Mill, Part I

*Week Six*

Someone once told me, during a gold rush, sell shovels. So when the Bitcoin/cryptocurrency fad took off, I decided not to invest in them. Instead, I built super-computers called "mining rigs" that harvested the digital currency. At the time, it seemed like a good idea. Build a few computers. Sell them to a few people. Make some money. And maybe, if I had time, I'd build another high-end rig for myself.

Here's how cryptomining works: much like the US dollar, you can only receive a piece of cryptocurrency by providing goods and services. After all, if they just handed them out, the currency would be worthless. There needs to be some sort of action that results in the awarding of a Bitcoin, or Ethereum, or Zcash, or whatever the crypto du jour is. So the way to "earn" cryptocurrency aside from just buying one is to "mine" it.

So how you do you mine something that's digital? Well - and this is the dumbed down version - you need a computer to solve a very difficult math problem. If it solves the problem, you get a piece of cryptocurrency. And these problems are tough. Your laptop won't be able to find the solution to these problems, at least not in a timely fashion. As a result, people realized that if you have a very powerful computer, you can solve these problems much quicker which results in more cryptocurrency.

Still following me? Great.

Now, how do you build a mining rig? To build a successful one - or, at least, a profitable one - you need to use high-end graphics processing units (GPUs) that are capable of performing millions and billions of computations per second. These will then take the cryptocurrency problems and find solutions quickly. The speed of which is called a "hashrate." Higher numbers = speedier solutions. Speedier solutions = more cryptocurrency.

The problem, or should I say "problems," with these GPUs is that they draw a tremendous amount of energy and as a result, they get very hot. "Good" mining rigs will have upwards of 6 of these bad boys running at a time. So not only will a mining rig destroy your electricity bill, but you need a serious cooling system to make sure they don't overheat. It comes down to finding a balance - your rig needs to be as quick as possible but not so quick that it draws too much energy and you lose money with high electric bills. This is why cryptomining is so popular in cold places like Iceland where they don't need to expend a lot of energy to cool off their rigs. Adding to all these difficulties, it's becoming increasingly harder to find GPUs that aren't marked up by some insane margin.

All set? Still following? Cool, cryptomining 101 is over.

I'd made a few rigs, sold some to friends, and watched as they started making hundreds if not thousands of dollars every month just by having their rigs run in the background. And when the cryptocurrency boom happened in late 2017, these numbers exploded as well. So it was time for me to dip my toe in the pond.

I named my rig *Wintermute* after an AI character in William Gibson's Neuromancer. The difference between *Wintermute* and the other rigs I built in the past was that I'd be using my 20 years of computer programming knowledge to Frankenstein 8 current GPUs so they'd hyperclock - they'd push my hashrates to incredible numbers while lapping the hashrates of standard NVIDIAs or AMDs. I based the chip programming on swarm intelligence, which saved time on duplicate functions, and allowed for the processing power to concentrate on new solutions.

Think of it like this: one bird flies in a direction and the others follow. By following, they form patterns that ripple out to the rest of the birds. This hive mind becomes - basically - a single organism that can evolve based on conditions. It gets interesting when you consider that each of those birds follows very simple rules, and there's no governing body telling the individual birds how to move. This leads the birds to develop intelligent global behavior which is unknown to each individual bird.

Translate those birds to billions of computer algorithms and you get a flock of them concentrating on finding the solution without needing to waste time doing duplicate functions. So while your top-end miner without my proprietary swarm intelligence programming was getting a hashrate of 32 MH/s, *Wintermute* was pulling in 66 MH/s and not drawing any more power than slower rigs.

The cryptomining community is welcoming, but when someone discovers a way to increase their hashrates by a point or two, they usually keep it to themselves. It's greedy, but having a quicker computer means you're taking that bit of cryptocurrency away from someone on a slower computer. Still, I couldn't help but brag a bit. Anonymously, I made a post to a message board indicating my hashrates. Calls of "bullshit" turned to calls of "genius" once I posted a copy of my mining log.

Still, *Wintermute* worked like a charm. I was pulling in around $900/month after paying my electric bill, and managed to throw that cash back into building duplicates of *Wintermute*. Six rigs in, and I was quickly running out of room and air conditioning.

---

The Peabody Mill was one of thousands of textile mills that dotted the New England landscape. Some of these were redeveloped into luxury condos, malls, or office spaces. Others, like the Peabody, fell into decay and became makeshift houses for the homeless, druggies, and wild animals. I'd first learned of the Peabody Mill when a friend and urban exploration enthusiast brought me through it. To him, it was just a stone building with graffiti and rotting wood beams. To me, it was perfect.

In one of the many oversights of our town's infrastructure and electrical grid, they never managed to turn off the power to the mill. But, since no one had actually used power at the mill in over two decades, it never showed up on any spreadsheets.

Free energy.

Plus, the mill was close enough to our downtown that I could pick up unsecured WIFI from a local business. And once I realized this, and felt how cool the brick and stone walls kept the building - even in the summer - I knew the mill was about to become the best place to run and store *Wintermute 1 - 6.*

I got to work on building a steel room with a triple locked door. A couple of welds, some high capacity fans, proper ventilation ducts, rubber seals to keep out flood waters and river rats, and I was ready to put it into the basement of the mill under the cover of night. Installing it was easy, and it was so deep and out of the way, that no one would ever know it was there. Plus, I ran the entire system on a Virtual Private Network (VPN) which made it look like all of *Wintermute's* internet usage was coming from somewhere in Montana. And even if someone did find it, they'd need an acetylene torch to get in.

Every two days, I'd stop by the mill and download my earnings to a digital removable wallet. This way, if I were hacked, or the machines were destroyed, I'd only lose two days' worth of cash. At the end of the first month, I'd pocketed a little over $6,000 with almost no overhead outside of the original rigs and the steel box. The next month, I made another $8,000. If this kept up, I'd clear $100,000+ by the end of the year. I was practically printing money.

---

My Saturday night was all planned out. I'd head to the Mill, download my latest earnings, and then head to dinner with friends. Having spent the better part of five months in my garage and a moldy mill, I was looking forward to a fancy night out. I bought a new dress for the occasion, bought some heels that added significant height to my 5'5" frame, and managed to look like a respectable human being for the first time in years. It's nice having some extra cash in your bank account.

Yes, I had to go to the Mill first. And because in my haste to leave my house, I'd forgotten a change of shoes, I'd have to slog through dirt and debris in my brand new shoes. Slightly bad planning on my part. But, I didn't want to head to the Mill after my evening was done. It'd be too dark, and I was planning on drinking a little more than necessary. Also, I'd missed yesterday's wallet download and I didn't want to go any more days without grabbing it.

I parked my car about a quarter of a mile down the road from the Mill. Best not to make anyone suspicious that there were strange things afoot. Of course, seeing a woman in a cocktail dress walking down the side of the road at dusk near a dilapidated building would probably set off a few alarms in the heads of the conservative citizens of my antique New England town.

The Mill was quiet. And having walked the path dozens of times since I installed *Wintermute,* I knew where I was going - even in the fading light. But once I got to the steel room that held *Wintermute,* I realized something was not right. The walls had been cut open, all six of my rigs were torn apart, and the motherboards were missing. Stranger still, the GPUs - the most expensive parts of the rigs - were still there. Maybe it was just some teenagers who needed to fulfill their strange desires to destroy things. Maybe it was some junkies who needed to sell something quick to get their fix. But what really concerned me was the methodical way they cut through the wall. Teenagers and junkies don't normally carry around angle grinders.

I couldn't call the cops, because even though cryptomining is not illegal, the whole "trespassing" business would land me in hot water. So, I took stock of everything. Cleaned it up as best I could, and walked out of the box with the intention to spend the next few days reprogramming new motherboards. And, figuring out a way to better secure *Wintermute.*

One step out into the basement and I felt it. Right into my back. Pressed hard up against the silk of my stupidly expensive dress. And having never been in this situation before, I was surprised I knew exactly what it was. A gun.

## The Mill, Part II

*Week Seven*

Consolidated Data Systems knows you. They know who you are. They know where you live. And, they know what you'll do next. Every time you use a credit card, swipe a loyalty card, or sign up for a company's newsletter, CDS adds to your profile. They then take this data and sell it back to companies who pay good money to have detailed insights into the types of people who are buying their products.

Through a series of management disasters, failed initiatives, and a souring of the public to this blatant rip-off of their privacy, CDS's stock has plummeted. More and more consumers are opting out of sharing their data, the federal government is cracking down on illegal use of private information, and CDS employees are jumping ship.

Just like a scared animal backed into a corner, CDS is willing to do anything to survive no matter the cost. The one thing they realize they do have is a tremendous amount of computing power. After all, studying/stealing everyone's purchasing habits throughout the globe requires the handling of a lot of data. And these days, just simply mentioning "cryptomining" in a press release will raise your share price by 10 points.

The one smart thing CDS did was realize they had all this computational power, and began researching how they could use it to cryptomine without much overhead. Convert their data centers to rows and rows of mining rigs and they'll churn out cryptocurrency at an unprecedented rate. Figure out a way to maximize the hashrates, and they'd own the world.

This is why I'm sitting in a dirty cocktail dress, shoeless, in the back of a black SUV headed to some remote location. Ted Jeffers, the head of security for CDS, was nice enough to hold a gun to my back when he asked me to follow him. Having been in an abandoned mill, at night, the scene was set for a "Missing Girl Movie of the Week." I was strangely relieved when he walked me to an SUV and told me to get inside. If someone isn't going to rape and kill you in ruined building, they're probably not going to rape or kill you at all. But the fact that he needed to use a gun to persuade me was still horribly unsettling.

After formally introducing himself to me, locking the car door, and putting the gun away, I felt I was entitled to a few questions.

"So... How did you find me?" I asked.

“We're CDS. We know more than you think. It started with that anonymous comment you made about your hashrates on the message board," Jeffers sneered.

I knew that would come back to bite me.

"That was tantalizing for us," Jeffers wiped his lower lip with his index finger, "From there, we looked at your logs, studied the GPUs you were using - their serial numbers - and who specifically bought them, in a corresponding time frame. We matched them up with other purchases you made, and figured out pretty quickly who you were. We looked at your energy bills, and realized the rig wasn't at your home. So we looked at WIFI spikes in the area, and wouldn't you know it, a coffee shop downtown had a really high internet usage. Too high for a normal shop. From there, we studied places that fell under the WIFI umbrella of the coffee shop. We knew you bought steel, locks, and most importantly, rubber seals. Those really gave away the fact that your rig was in a location prone to flooding. Hence, the Peabody Mill."

"Jesus. Privacy really is dead."

"You have no idea."

"So, why the gun? Couldn't you have just called? Asked me to participate."

"Nope. Again, we know exactly who you are. You listen to *Rage Against the Machine, N.W.A.,* and *Cypress Hill.* You own a can of mace. You've taken shooting lessons in the past five years. You actively post in protest groups on Reddit. You subscribe to several anarchist newsletters."

"*Martha Stewart Living* is anarchist?"

"Funny. But yeah, based on those purchases, we determined you weren't someone who'd come along quietly."

"Why didn't you just reverse engineer my motherboards? Steal my programing software? You don't need me."

"We tried that. Turns out the one thing we couldn't crack were the security measures you'd programmed in."

A smile ran across my face. He was talking about a little security protocol I'd thrown into my code. If the software determined that someone was tampering with it, it would "brick" the motherboard. Basically, it erased everything.

"So what do you expect me to do? Program your rigs? Watch you collect millions of dollars?"

"Well, we intend to fully compensate you for your programming efforts."

"And what's to stop me from going to the police? Telling them you kidnapped me?"

"Go for it. Tell them everything. I'm sure they'd love to hear how an upstanding public company kidnapped you to program their computers. They'll have you committed in less than a day."

"And how long is this going to take? You know," I pointed to my dress, "This isn't really my everyday attire."

"We've already contacted your friends, and left messages saying you weren't feeling well."

"And they believed you?"

"No. They believed you."

"They believed me?"

"Audio spoofing."

I shifted uncomfortably in my seat. CDS had thought of almost everything.

"We expect, with your background, you'll be able to insert your code into our system in less than a day. Send your program out to all of our mining rigs. And with any luck, you'll be back home tomorrow."

---

I looked at my bank account. A deposit of $250,000 from CDS sat intimidatingly at the top of the page. Further proof that I was "working" for them. No one would believe I'd been kidnapped if they'd paid me a quarter of a million dollars to program their computers. It'd been six weeks since Jeffers had pulled me out of the mill. I hadn't been back to clean up the remnants of *Wintermute*, nor to pick up my shoes that had fallen off as I was "escorted" out of the building.

According to the reports I'd set up, my swarm programming was working well for CDS. They were pulling in half a million dollars a month. Their mining rigs, situated in five different "farms" around the country, were churning day and night. Each was running my code, and the entire setup was quickly outpacing any other setup like it in the world. They'd even told investors that their new cryptomining endeavor utilizing a distinct program developed "in-house" was quickly turning it into an industry leader. Their stock price jumped, and I imagined all of the executives patting each other on their backs for all of their "hard work."

But I waited, because I knew.

Giving someone free-access to an internal computer system is stupid. Giving someone with an extensive knowledge of computer programing was downright disastrous, especially after you've held them at gunpoint and forced them to work. You'd think a company that specialized in breaking security would have put more measures in place. But they were frothing, and they were too excited to see those dollar signs start appearing on their bank sheets. So I waited. I needed them to see the fruits of my labor. I needed them to start reaping the benefits. I needed them to trust my code and not shut down any of their rigs. And once they did start reaping the benefits, I waited for the inevitable.

There were over 5,000 CDS mining rigs spinning away. Each had 8 GPUs per rig, and each GPU had a dedicated fan cooling it off.

If someone was looking at the rig monitors at around 4:30 in the morning on October 25, they would have seen it. The screens going blank, and a text readout saying, "Wintermute Lives" scrolling up them. Behind the scenes, they would have missed the large transaction that transferred the entirety of their latest cryptomining earnings to an external digital wallet that was attached to a small computer, in a small house, in a small New England town. And that pesky code I wrote that Jeffers had been so upset by - the code that bricked all my data? That code was about to run through all of CDS's computers, effectively wiping out all of the consumer profiles they'd stolen from every single person in the country.

But there was one other thing. One more command that was key to my plan.

*"fan=0"*

That was my favorite part. Assign the fan speed a value of 0. A short command line that told every fan on every GPU to turn off. But the thing was, there was nothing telling the GPUs to shut down. No, they'd continue to run. And run. And run. But without anything to cool them off, they'd overheat, meltdown, and destroy all of CDS's server farms. Scorched earth.

---

CDS claimed faulty wiring caused the "issues" at their server farms. That they'd be back up and running in a matter of days. But after two weeks, and with a stock price dipping into the single digits, CDS was forced to reveal that they'd lost all of their data - including the data stored on their redundant storage devices. Everything had been wiped out, and they were declaring bankruptcy.

When Jeffers and his cronies at CDS were figuring out who I was by studying my past purchases, they missed one key item. I'd purchased a *Nest Cam* to monitor *Wintermute*. Placed in an unassuming corner of the basement of the mill, it recorded everything in daylight and night vision and saved the past 30 days of footage to the cloud. As powerful as CDS was, they didn't put that together. And, accordingly, a clip of Jeffers holding a young woman in a dress at gunpoint made its way to our local police department through an anonymous source, and he was soon awaiting trial behind bars.

With cryptocurrency still trying to find its equilibrium, I decided it was time to exit the game. I never bothered rebuilding *Wintermute*. I'm sure someone could have made a nice chunk of change if they had found the rig and realized how expensive those GPUs were. But my time with cryptocurrency had come to an end. And truthfully, I had other things I wanted to concentrate on. With my new-found wealth, I was determined to continue to fight the CDSs of the world - those companies who prey on people (both figuratively and literally). So, I got to work building again. Creating something larger. Something even more powerful than a hyperclocked mining rig. I was putting together the initial plans of a computer science school to be built in a soon-to-be refurbished mill I'd just purchased.

# Divine Providence

*Week Eight*

Jason's ever-expanding gut overlapped the counter by less than an inch. Still, he made a note that - if he found the time - he'd start running again. He looked down at the microwave in his office's kitchen, and noticed that his colleague who'd used it previously didn't "cancel" off the remaining seconds on the screen. Jason sighed, pressed "cancel," and placed his frozen lasagna into the machine.

"Jay, how was the weekend man?" Ted asked, knowing full well how Jason's weekend went. Jason didn't even bother to look up from his rapidly cooking meat and cheese to acknowledge Ted's presence in the kitchen.

"Good. Can't complain. Went to the-"

"Listen," Ted being more important Ted, "Do you have the latest sales sheets for the northwest region? I want to get those in front of some of our distributors."

"Yeah, I'll send them once I'm done with lunch."

"See man, the thing is, I kinda need them now."

Jason looked at the remaining minutes on the microwave. 4:32. His shoulders fell in defeat and resignation.

"Yep," and he walked back to his cubicle to send Ted the Bastard his sales sheets.

Once back in the kitchen, Jason saw Judy standing in front of the microwave. Jason's partially-heated lasagna sat on top of it.

"Oh, sorry Jason. Was this yours?" Judy pointed to the quickly-cooling lunch, "I didn't know if this was someone's or whatever. Another minute or two and it'll be cooked."

Jason didn't even bother answering or fighting. He was rapidly losing all control in his life, and he had neither the strength nor the energy to try and take the wheel back.

---

Jason's head was pressed into the pillow. He could hear Marie somewhere back in the distance crashing clothes into the bottom of her bag in attempt to make sure he was both awake and aware of her displeasure.

"...and the thing is," an audible continuation on Marie's internal thoughts, "you just don't care anymore. You have no ambition. You don't even try anymore."

Jason closed his eyes and found comfort in the back of his eyelids.

"So that's it?" Marie again, "You have nothing to say?"

Jason remained motionless.

"Have a nice fucking life!" And Marie slammed the door to his bedroom. She heard her stomp down the stairs.

Out loud, Jason said, "Wait for it..."

And while she stood directly in front of the front door, Marie said, "I'm really leaving!"

"There it is" said Jason in a whisper. Another slammed door, followed by a car peeling out. Jason pulled the covers up to his neck, and, for the first time in a long time, found some relief.

---

The phone said "Mom" and Jason prepared himself. She only called with bad news. Usually, it was the death of an obscure relative or someone from her mall walkers group. Jason hoped it wasn't the dog. Not only did he genuinely like his mom's pet bijon, but without Ralphie to talk to, Jason knew his mom would call him more frequently.

"Hi, mom," Jason wondered if she could detect the subtle annoyance in his voice, "what's up?"

"Jason, there are people outside my house," she said without proper introduction.

"What kind of people? Salesmen? Religious people?"

"No. People. People people."

Jason had heard stories about people who live alone. How they begin to invent stories and draw connections that don't exist.

"Tell me about these people, mom."

"They're just standing there."

"Well, are they lost?"

"No. Well, I don't know. Maybe they're lost. But I think they're government spies."

"Government spies. Right. And why is the government spying on you, mom?"

"I bought something from Amazon. I think the government thinks I'm a terrorist. You know they're watching, right?"

"Uh, what did you buy on Amazon, mom?"

"I bought a new spade for my garden. I bet they think it's a weapon."

"Mom, I seriously doubt the government thinks a 70 year-old divorcee in suburbia with a *mahjongg* hobby is going to bring down society with a garden shovel."

"You never know honey. Oh wait, now they're taking pictures of each other. Why are they taking pictures of my house?"

"Maybe they like your roses. Maybe, and hear me out on this, maybe they're taking pictures of themselves and using your house as a backdrop."

"You could be right."

"Do me a favor, let me know if they come back."

"I will. Thanks honey. Oh, by the way, do you and Marie want to come by for Sunday dinner?"

"No mom. Marie and I broke up."

"What? Why? What did you do this time?"

Jason rubbed his eyes. He needed to get off the phone. "Mom, I didn't want to tell you this, but Marie used to kill drifters."

---

The bar was lit by one-too-many neon signs, creating a white glow that lit the dirty corners a bit too well. Jason sat at the bar with a tall glass of beer. Next to him sat his best friend Matt, who, if it were possible, was even less ambitious than Jason.

"Marie was so obsessed with changing you that," Matt struggled to use the right words, "you know, she was just a bitch man."

"Don't say that," Jason twisted the beer in front of him, "she's not a bitch."

"She wanted you to be her ideal man. But you know what I think? I think what she really wanted was for you to save her."

The front door opened in the distance. Jason didn't lift his head to see who walked into the bar. Matt hit him on the shoulder and casually pointed his chin to the door. "Two smoke shows just walked in. The best way to get over a breakup is to make really bad decisions. And these girls look like the best worst decisions."

"OK. We'll, I've got to piss. Try not to end up on a watch list while I'm gone."

As Jason walked to the restroom, Matt yelled over his shoulder, "Hey Jason, if you're American before you go into the bathroom and you're American when you come out of the bathroom, what are you while you're in the bathroom?"

Jason didn't even bother to answer.

"European!"

Jason cracked a smile.

---

Matt was deep in conversation with the two girls when Jason came out of the bathroom. Jason looked around to make sure he was in the right place. Matt, after all, decorated his apartment with vintage *G.I. Joes,* hadn't had a girlfriend since ever, and would list the last time he showered as "questionable."

"Jason! Come here, I'd like you to meet-" and before Matt could finish, the girls came running over to Jason and hugged him tightly, "uh... this is Kate and Nova."

Jason pried them off of him, and saw one of the girls crying.

"Hey, uh... what's uh... what's up? Did I hear that right? Nova?" Jason studied the girls. The one who wasn't crying said, "Yeah, it's like Supernova, and trust me, I'm just as hot."

Jason looked at Matt as Matt happily mouthed, "What. The Fuck." with the biggest smile he'd ever seen on his friend. Kate was still crying, while Nova asked them what they were up to.

"I was just heading out," said Jason, pulling out his wallet.

"You can't go!" cried Kate, "Please! Please don't go! We've come so far to see you!"

Jason gave her an odd and confused glance. "Yeah, I'm out."

He put a 20 on the bar, gulped down the remainder of his beer, and bid Matt and the ladies a good night. Kate tried to grab his hand, almost to the point of obsession, but he quickly pulled it away, tucked it in his pocket, and walked briskly out of the bar.

---

First voicemail, "Jason, holy shit dude. These chicks are insane. You should have stayed. Things got amazing. It's like they just wanted to ... be near me. I don't know. It was weird. But the really crazy part was, they kept talking like they knew us. They knew too much about us. They could've boiled my rabbit for all I care, they were hot as fuck! Oh yeah, it's Matt. Call me back. They want to see you again."

Second voicemail, "Jason, it's Marie. I don't know if you think you're funny or what, but that was uncool. You don't have the motivation to clean up your life, but you do have the motivation to hire actors to follow me around and spit on me? Fuck you."

Marie was losing it. Matt might have been losing it too. Jason shrugged both of them off, got out of bed, and walked down to his kitchen. He caught a brief glimpse of them out his window. Four... no, five people standing on the sidewalk outside of his house. Some were taking pictures, others were genuflecting toward his house. He pulled the slats of his blinds down and peered out to get a better look. There was something odd about them - outside of the fact that they set up shop on a sidewalk and were taking pictures of his house while seemingly praying.

Jason thought he may have been too hard on his mom.

He quickly assembled breakfast, took a quick shower, and opened his front door to head out to work. But instead of being greeted with his front porch, he was hit with an avalanche of items falling on him. There were baked good, candles, pictures of children, and a symbol of three interlocking rings in the shape of a triangle on pieces of wood and paper.

He gathered all of the items together, placed them in a neat pile on his porch, and began walking to his car. One of the people who were still on the sidewalk taking pictures shouted, "There he is!"

All five people began running toward Jason. He, in turn, began running at full sprint toward his car. Fumbling for his keys, he made it just inside his car before the mob caught up with him. Some pressed their hands up to the windows, others made an attempt to open his doors. Jason honked his horn and managed to reverse his car into the street and drive away. In his rearview mirror, he saw all of the people on their knees, praying in a circle while looking up at the sky.

---

Still shaking from being attacked, Jason walked into his job at *Smithson Prefabricated Homes* with an uneasy edge. He was greeted by Judy who informed him that several people had already stopped by to see him, but none left their names.

Strange, he didn't have any appointments today.

Opening up his laptop, his emails began flooding in.

*Dude, call me. Women are showing up at my doorstep. Ok, there are some dudes in the mix too. But all of them want to talk with me. Some asked me to preach to them. One woman said she wanted me to impregnate her. They won't stop talking about you. What the hell is going on? Did you sign up for a Russian bride?*
*-Matt*

*Jason,*
*I'm calling the cops. This isn't funny. Call off your hounds.*
*-Marie*

*Jason,*
*It's your neighbor Andrew from across the street. There are like 30 or 40 people gathered on your front lawn. I don't know if you're having a BBQ or something, but at this point it's becoming a disturbance. Our HOA doesn't allow more than 20 people on a lawn at the same time.*

Jason sat back in his chair. His life had officially gone off the rails. He expected to either wake up, or find a camera crew hiding around the corner ready to unveil that he'd been on a prank show. Neither happened.

"Jason, this is Judy at the front desk." Jason's phone sprang to life, "There's about 8 or 9 people here who want to talk with you."

Jason peered over his cubicle and saw a group of people in the lobby. Some held signs. Others had gifts. One had a painted picture of Jason, albeit one that removed his gut, his wrinkles, his bald spot, and the grey hair on his temples. And there, amid the chaos, was that same triangle made up of three rings.

"Thanks Judy. Tell them I'll be right out."

Jason didn't even bother hanging up the phone. He ducked behind his row of cubicles, and sprinted for the back stairway. He ran into the parking lot and saw a line of people 100 bodies deep waiting to get into the building. He ducked behind a bush and spotted his car in the distance. It, too, was covered with candles, gifts, and the symbol.

Instead, Jason ran in the opposite direction, away from the line of people and nowhere near his car. Hopping a fence, he found himself in a line of woods that separated the residential part of town from the commercial corridor.

"Matt!" Jason whisper yelled into his phone, "I need to meet up with you."

"Jason, am I glad you called," Jason could hear a party happening in the background, "these people are saying some wild shit about you. Like, crazy shit. I think they're part of a sex cult or something."

"Great. I need you to meet me at the *Bethel Motor Inn*. Come alone and don't tell anyone where you're going."

"Yeah. You got it."

Jason rang his mother, "Mom, it's Jason."

"Jason! I was just having a brunch with some people who say they know you."

"Mom. Get them out of your house. Lock your doors. Close your windows. Don't answer the phone unless it's me."

"But they're really nice people. And, they brought gifts!"

"Mom. I'll call you later. Get them out of the house."

The last call was going to be the hardest to make. "Marie. Hey, it's Ja-"

"Fuck you. Fuck you! Jason, someone threw a rock at me. A goddamned rock! And once it slammed into my arm, they came over and said I was evil incarnate and you were a being of light. What the hell is going on with you, Jason?"

"I... I don't know. I really don't. I'm trying to figure it out. But do me a favor..."

"You want me to do you a favor? How about you kiss my ass?"

"Marie. Please. It's important. I don't know who these people are, but I think you're in danger."

"You *think* I'm in danger? Oh, having a rock tossed at me didn't convince you? Being spit on my strangers didn't convince you?"

"OK. I *know* you're in danger. I'm headed to the *Bethel Motor Inn*. Matt is meeting me there. We're going to figure this out. I think it'd be best if you met us there."

Click.

"Shit."

---

The *Bethel Motor Inn* was a representation of a better time; a time when motels weren't looked upon as havens for druggies, prostitutes and near-homeless families. Built with the intention of offering travelers a place to rest en route to their final destinations, the *Bethel Motor Inn*, sadly, now represented the final destination for too many people.

Jason, still sweaty from his run to the Inn, grabbed his room key and walked into his room. Immediately, he drew the shades, sat on the bed, and rubbed his temples. *What the hell was going on?*

His phone beeped with a text message from Matt. "Which room, homey?"

"202"

30 seconds later, Matt was at the door, and Matt had brought Nova.

"Dude. I told you. Come alone," Jason said, while glaring at Nova.

"Yeah, but Nova is cool."

Jason peered around, and grabbed both Matt and Nova and brought them inside.

"Nova," Jason said, desperately trying to grasp at sanity, "can you please tell me what's happening. Why are people following me? Are you part of this? And what is ... this?"

Nova's eyes grew wide, "Holy shit. Holy shit! I'm the harbinger. I'm the motherfucking harbinger! I mean, you read about these people, but you never expect the stories to be about you."

"What are you talking about?"

"Yeah, what does 'harbinger' mean?" Matt asked.

Tears were forming in Nova's eyes. "I can't believe this. I'm the one."

"The one what!?" Jason's voice wavered between confusion and annoyance.

"I'm the one who gets to tell you about your destiny."

"Ok. Leave. Get out. Go." Jason walked to the hotel room door and opened it up. Standing in the doorway was Marie. "Marie, uh... I didn't think you'd show up. Get in." He pulled her inside the room and she sat down on the bed opposite Matt and Nova. Jason paced the room. Nova glared at Marie.

"Jason. What is going on. And who is Matt's girlfriend? Oh, quick follow-up, why does Matt's girlfriend look like she's about to stab me in the eye with a hotel pen?" asked Marie, clearly sick of all that was happening to her.

"Funny enough, Nova-"

"Nova?" interjected Marie.

"Yes, Nova was about to tell us. Turns out, she's the harbinger."

"Well why the fuck not? Come Nova, tell us what the hell is going on,"

"Oh my god! Ok, well first," Nova quickly looked around the room, "I need to make this more formal." She walked into the bathroom and came out with a cheap motel bathrobe draped over her shoulders like a cape. Next, she gestured for Matt to sit down. Standing in front of all three of them, she began to talk.

"I'm from the year 2348-"

Marie stood up to walk out the door.

"Please. Sit. Please. I'll explain everything," Nova pleaded. This concerns you too. "In the future, we've developed a means of time travel. We can go forward and back through time, but because it takes so much power to travel back and forth, we can only go so far."

"And why did you choose to come back to 2018?" asked Jason.

"This was the earliest time we could travel to," Nova the harbinger said.

"OK, but what's with all the people following me? Who are they? What do they want with me?"

"Jason, you are our savior. You create a religion that brings peace and harmony to the world. You are a divine being who sheds light on the darkness."

"Lady, you've got the wrong guy," Marie interrupted. "Jason can't even remember to do the dishes in his sink."

"No. We've come all this way to help Jason start his church," Nova turned to Jason, "To show you the way."

"I'm sorry, and please forgive me if this is off-base, but are you part of a cult?" Jason asked, "You know... brainwashed?"

"No. I'm a follower, like millions of others across the world, of the Fellowship of Man. A religion started by you, Jason, in the year 2018."

"Get the fuck out of here!" said Matt, finally. Jason was trying to process all of this, while Marie was still filled with disbelief. "So if Jason is some magical god, who the hell am I?"

"You, Matt, are his apostle. You spread Jason's message throughout the world. You preach the word of the one true god to all who will listen."

"OK. This has been fun. Little Miss Hippy Chick has apparently taken one too many hits of *Molly* at the last *Phish* concert she went to." Marie got up to leave.

"And she," Nova pointed at Marie, "Is the disbeliever. The darkness. The one who tries to thwart Jason's lightness."

"Well, I hope in whatever bible they write about all of this, they get this next part right," and Marie extended her middle finger to Nova. "I'm out!" Marie opened the door and stopped suddenly.

The parking lot of the *Bethel Motor Inn* was filled with thousands and thousands of people. All stared intently at the door to room 202, waiting for Jason to appear. Marie slowly stepped back inside.

"Jason," Marie said, slightly astonished, "Your people await."

"Everyone stop! This is fucking ridiculous. You," he pointed a finger at Nova, "and this... cult or whatever, are full of shit. I'm not religious. I haven't been to church since I chugged all that communion wine in eighth grade. Plus, and hear me out on this, time travel doesn't exist."

"Yet," Nova interjected.

"You know," Matt said, "You don't need to believe in anything to lead a religion. You just need to make others believe that you believe. All great religious leaders know they're peddling snake oil."

Marie sat back down. The chanting outside grew louder. Jason turned to Nova.

"So tell me future girl, why me? What makes me so divine?"

"Well, as our texts have taught us, you have always helped the needy."

"I volunteered at a homeless shelter once because the girl who organized it was hot."

"It is said that you have the ability to resurrect man and animal alike."

"Ha!" Matt suddenly chimed in, "She said 'erect!'"

"Resurrect? Sorry Nova, I've never resurrected anything."

"Our texts speak of the time you brought life to that child at Currituck Beach."

"Currituck? No, that was... that was CPR. I was a lifeguard."

"Congrats Jason, you're just a normal lifeguard," Marie tapped him on the shoulder. Outside, a chorus began singing.

"Most importantly, you were visited by an angel of light on your 10th birthday who recognized your divinity."

"My 10th birthday? Nova, I'm sorry, but your 'texts' are just exaggerations. These are embellishments to make me seem more important."

"Why? What happened on your 10th birthday?" Marie, suddenly curious.

"It was nothing. My parents had already split up. My mom left me with my dad, and my dad's new girlfriend gave me a copy of *Led Zeppelin's* fourth album. I only remember it because it was the only gift I got that year."

"She was an angel," Nova said reverently.

"No, she was a prostitute he met in Vegas."

The sun was falling deeper and deeper in the sky. The streetlights turned on, and the parking lot of the *Bethel Motor Inn* was filled with swaying constellations from the candles held by Jason's followers.

Defeated, resigned, but intrigued, Jason realized he couldn't escape. There was only one door out of the room, and the crowd outside grew more and more energized the longer he waited.

"What the hell am I supposed to say to these people?"

"You are a divine being of light. Speak from your heart." Nova said.

"This better not end with me nailed to a cross." Jason let out a sigh and stood up.

"Say something about how I'm a sex god and all hot chicks should procreate with me," Matt said, way too seriously.

Jason straightened his hair in the mirror and noticed for the first time today a design on his t-shirt. He was wearing a *Led Zeppelin* shirt with the four "runes" featured on the band's fourth album. Seeing the three circles in the triangle formation used by drummer John Bonham, Jason let out a laugh. He turned to Marie.

"How do I look?"

"Like a guy who has absolutely no idea what he's doing."

"So... normal. Got it."

---

Jason slowly made his way out, and stood in front of the mass of people. It took him a few moments to calm his nerves and find the appropriate cadence. But once he kicked into gear, the people were enthralled. He welcomed them, thanked them, and talked about his desire to find control in a world quickly spinning into chaos. Still inside the room and still filled with incredulity, Marie watched as Jason commanded the crowd. He was kind, warm, and important. And despite what she'd thought of him in the past, she had to admit that this was the most ambitious thing she'd ever seen Jason do.

## Delivery

### *Week Nine*

The clouds always seem bigger in Italy. They have more weight, more texture, and seem to pull you with their movement. Davidson watched as they rippled over Rome, turning the city into a patchwork of sun and shadow. He poured himself another glass from the bottle of *2003 Château Latour Grand Vin*, and smiled at the silent disgust the waiter had shared as he brought a non-Italian wine for this strange American. He held the wine by the stem, and remarked at how well the red of the wine contrasted with the greens, blues, oranges, and yellows of the city.

The *Rome Cavalier*i sits pressed into the side of *Monte Mario*, and stands like a long slumbering giant overlooking his empire. From his perch on the balcony of the hotel, Davidson took a deep breath and looked at his watch. It should have happened by now.

Deep in the city below, a man held a package in his satchel, and was running through the crowds of tourists in *Piazza Navona*. While they stopped to admire the *Fountain of the Four Rivers - The Fontana dei Fiumi* - his eyes were on the ground, deftly weaving in and out of footsteps and avoiding tripping on the scalloped cobblestones of the street. Reaching the northern end of the Piazza, he looked at his watch and let out a deep breath. He was late.

Kate sat on the wall of the *Ponte Umberto I*, and watched as the green waters of the Tiber moved beneath. Whenever she travelled internationally - for business or pleasure - she purposefully tried to look as un-American as possible. For the past few decades, citizens from Kate's home country had left a stain throughout the world, and she detested them for it. Americans were loud, self-centered, wore overstated clothing, and expected to be treated like *McDonalds* consuming royalty wherever they went. When Kate was mistaken for someone from another country, she took it as a compliment.

She'd left her watch and camera back at the hotel - preferring instead to take pictures by memory. And this spot on the River Tiber was the perfect place to take in the afternoon sun and feel a warm wind fly through her long blonde hair. She'd remember this moment always, closed her eyes, felt her chest rise with a breath, and exhaled a long slow breath.

Davidson took out his phone and placed it on the table next to his glass of wine. He stared at it, waiting for it to ring. In his line of work, he preferred to be the man behind the scenes, he never opted for the dirty work. But with time ticking away, he wondered if he'd have to head into town and do this himself.

The man with the satchel wiped sweat off his brow. His feet hurt from running on the uneven streets, and the swaying balance of the satchel had ignited his side. He'd made it to the bridge. He turned right to walk down the stairs toward the riverbank, but not before catching a stunning blonde sitting on the side of the bridge busy being lost to the world.

At the bottom of the stairs, the temperature was markedly cooler, as if the water sucked the heat from the air. His eyes darted back and forth, trying to locate his point man. With relief, he saw a distinctive man walking toward him. He was tall in a white suit wearing dark sunglasses and a brimmed hat, and he angrily pointed at his watch.

"Are you Edward?" the man with the satchel asked in elongated vowels typical of an Italian working through the English language.

"I am, and you're late," said Edward, his hand already outstretched to receive the package.

The man reached into his satchel and pulled out the package carefully rolled in protective wrap. He gingerly handed it to Edward. The man with the satchel was never told what was inside each package. This allowed for plausible deniability, and made him more comfortable not knowing how dangerous or illegal his bag's contents were as he ran through the crowds of Rome.

Edward carefully unwrapped the package and stared inside. The man with the satchel craned his neck as he attempted to take a peek, but Edward closed it tightly.

"Tell your boss you did well," said Edward with a tip of his hat, "Thank you."

On the bridge, Kate felt a tap on her shoulder. "Excuse me," it was an American tourist putting on an exaggerated accent to "help" with translation, "Would you take a photo of my wife and I?" The tourist pointed to his camera. Kate smiled - her disguise had worked.

"Of course," smiled Kate, in unadulterated American English.

Finally up the stairs and at street level, Edward spotted her. Her back was to him, and she was in a slight crouch - the unmistakable body position of someone taking a photo. He tossed the torn wrapping into a nearby trash can and double checked the item in his hand.

A few miles away, Davidson's phone began vibrating on the table.

Walking toward her, Edward felt a pit form in his stomach. She hadn't seen him yet, and this was probably for the best. In matters like this, he preferred the element of surprise.

Kate handed the camera back to the tourists, smiled, and turned back to the river. Looking north, she made a mental note to Google where the source of the Tiber was located when she got back to the hotel.

Edward took a deep breath, and placed a hand on Kate's lower back.

"Don't jump," he said.

Still staring out over the river, Kate didn't turn to him, "If I had to wait any longer, I might have."

Edward took the item out from around his back, and placed it on the wall in front of her.

"What is this?"

"It's my excuse."

Kate tucked her long hair behind her ears, and for the first time turned toward Edward.

"How dangerous is this?"

"Extremely."

Kate took the lacquered wooden box off the wall and, for the first time all day, felt her pulse rise. A smile formed at the corner of her lips, and peaked somewhere below her nose. Even before she opened it, she knew what it was.

"I have delivered the package," the man with the satchel said into the phone. He looked back over his shoulder and saw Edward talking with the blonde on the bridge.

"Excellent. I've transferred funds to your account," said Davidson before hanging up the phone.

Kate slowly opened the box and found her great-grandmother's engagement ring sitting squarely inside. The late afternoon sun worked its way through the prisms of the diamond and cast rainbows on the inside of the box. Finally, she turned back to Edward who had already gotten on one knee.

If it weren't for the billowy clouds rolling through the sky, Davidson would have thought he were looking out over a painting. He followed the serpentine line of the Tiber down toward the outline of the *Corte Suprema di Cassazione*, which sat just on the other side of Kate and Edward's bridge. He raised a glass in their direction, took a long sip, and placed it back on the table.

# Never Say Die

## *Week Ten*

The *clank* came first. An auditory signal that the ocean depths were exploring the structural vulnerabilities of the unmanned underwater vehicle. *Donner*, as it was known by the crew, was descending toward the *Axial Seamount*, a newly-formed underwater volcano several hundred miles off the Oregon coast. Thousands of feet above the *Donner* on the surface of the Pacific Ocean, the *R.V. Matuszak* rolled gently over the open-ocean waves. Inside, a crowd of people stared at a wall of screens waiting to catch the first glimpse of their target.

*Benthic Labs* had been researching the volcano and the plume of organic life that came with it for the better part of a year. *Donner* and its sister UUV *Blitzen* would make several trips a week down to the ocean floor, collect samples, and bring them back to the *Matuszak* for study. But it was their discovery over a month ago that changed everything. A quick mention of their find in several local papers throughout Portland and Astoria, and *Benthic Labs* suddenly found their funding increased tenfold. Private investors, museums, and, strangely, a commercial real estate company, had thrown serious cash at the small research firm.

The UUV control room inside the *Matuszak* was awash in red light. On one wall, six different monitors played live feeds from the cameras attached to *Donner* some 4,000 feet below them. Save for the typical grey ocean detritus that swirled in front of the cameras, the screens were mostly a deep indigo.

Jake Carnes, the UUV technician, dove the *Donner* deeper and deeper, as a readout on a screen ticked off each 10 foot interval. With the advent of GPS, it was becoming increasingly easier to find and re-find objects throughout the ocean. Carnes knew if he followed the point on his digital readout, he'd more or less land within a few feet of the target.

In the back of the room, a man tapped the pads of his fingertips together - waiting. He'd come aboard at the behest of the new investors, never introduced himself to the crew, and was growing more and more impatient. The fact that he wore a suit onboard a working research vessel told the crew all they needed to know: this guy was not only out of his element, he was, more than likely, a giant douche.

"We should be coming up on it now," said Carnes, his eyes darting across the various screens looking for the first sign.

The man in the suit sat forward in his seat. A radar readout on one screen showed that whatever this object was, it was huge.

*Donner's* bow light caught it first, a giant wooden structure so large, it seemed to pull everyone in the room toward it. As the cloud kicked up by *Donner's* thrusters settled down, the rest of the object came into a view. Sitting on its side were the silted and deteriorated remains of a 17th century sailing ship. Carnes pushed *Donner* back and down the side of object until it ran down the stern nameplate. Thousands of feet above the wreck, the group saw the word "INFERNO" slide across their monitors. For the first time all day, the man in the suit smiled.

---

Guillermo Pérez, a notorious Spanish pirate known throughout the world for his violent temper and his namesake birth defect, had amassed a small fortune through systematic plundering of ships crossing the Atlantic en route to the colonies. In the holds of his two ships, he held enough treasure to purchase a navy. But unlike other pirates who spent their ill-gotten gains in ports throughout the Americas and Caribbean, Pérez's greed forced him to hoard all of it. He paid his crew just enough to keep them from mutiny, and only spent his plunder on improvements for his ships. As such, the *Halcón*, and Pérez's flagship, the *Inferno*, were some of the fastest and most feared ships to sail the seas.

Pérez assumed the British armada wouldn't pursue him around Cape Horn. The waters were too unpredictable, and despite the vast fortune onboard Pérez's ships, it wasn't worth the risk. The British, however, thought differently. Through his pirating endeavors, Pérez had procured a staggering amount of treasure, including priceless items seized from the holds of British ships. One item in particular, the *Crown of Leamington* - a present to the Governor of the Massachusetts Bay Colony - sat in an unassuming pile in the hold of the *Halcón*.

So valuable was the *Crown of Leamington*, that the British were told to take it back by any means necessary. And so, they took the risk of sailing through the waters of Tierra Del Fuego after Pérez.

To his credit, Pérez managed to lead the British on a months-long chase up the western coast of South America and Mexico. But with his crew tired, and his ships in need of supplies, the British were quickly closing open water by the time Pérez had made it to Point Conception off the California coast. In an effort to distract and confuse the British, he ordered the crew of the *Halcón* to sail into the protected waters of Morro Bay, while the *Inferno* continued its route north.

The British, realizing the deception, but assuming the Crown were held in the *Inferno*, continued on. The fate of the *Halcón* has remained a mystery for the past several hundred years. Some claim they pursued the British and watched as Pérez and the *Inferno* were inundated with cannon fire, causing the sea cliffs in a small harbor on the Oregon coast to cave in around the ship. Others believe the crew of the *Halcón* purposely sank the ship somewhere along the jagged coastline of Big Sur - leaving its fabled treasure to churn below the rough seas.

But Pérez, not willing to have his riches fall into the hands of the British or into the deep abyss of the sea, had other plans. And so, as the feared Pirate Captain, Guillermo Pérez, also known by his long-hated nickname "One-Eyed Willy," instructed his men to dig tunnels to make their way out of the grotto the British armada had created around them, enacted his established protocol should he ever be separated from the *Halcón*.

Guillermo "One-Eyed Willy" Pérez never made it out of the cave. But on a tablet in the hold of the *Inferno*, he chiseled in a complex puzzle that would lead to the location of the *Halcón*.

---

Troy Perkins walked to the monitors in the control room of the *Matuszak*. He straightened his tie, and flattened his suit.

"There. That's where we're going," he said, pointing a finger at a gaping hole torn into the side of the Inferno when it sank some 30 years ago. One-

Eyed Willy's treasure had been nothing but a thorn in his side since its discovery by a group of kids a few decades ago. Through a series of events, it prevented his father's company from foreclosing on several properties and building a luxury golf course in their place. Instead, the company floundered, and it wasn't until Troy took over for his father a few years ago that he was able to begin to right the ship.

Now, aboard the *Matuszak* on an expedition his company helped fund, the tide was about to turn. Not only would he collect the remaining treasure from the *Inferno*, but he'd finally learn the location and fate of the *Halcón* and take that treasure for himself, too. Troy Perkins pushed Carnes' hand out of the way, and drove *Donner* through the hole in the side of the ship and into the dark future beyond.

# Panicked

*Week Eleven*

Mental illness runs through my family like the Nile through Egypt. And as I made my way through my 20s, I was thankful that I'd somehow avoided the curse. I'd seen it first hand, I knew of the seriousness of it all, the ways it can destroy people and families, and how despite it's very real dangers, no one talked about it. No one. It was swept under the rug. Sure, in closed circles someone might mention something out of earshot of others. They might blame an action or mistake on the illness. But when it came to a real and frank discussion, mental illness was never spoken about.

But as I sat on the floor of my bedroom in my apartment on the Upper East Side, rocking back and forth with my arms wrapped around my legs telling myself, "you're better than this," over and over again, I knew something was wrong. But, I assumed it was physical rather than mental. The reason I couldn't leave my apartment was because something was physically wrong with me. I'd had too much caffeine. I hadn't exercised in a while. I'd eaten some bad food.

My girlfriend at the time would grow angry with me because my fear of large crowds was growing steadily. So going to bars and clubs was out. Visiting her in Brooklyn took an incredible amount of energy, because it meant crowding myself into a subway train for 45 minutes. But I never had the strength to tell her *why*. Only that I couldn't.

And it continued to grow. I couldn't be anywhere without an easy exit. I needed a bathroom within a minute's reach. When I managed to will myself out of my apartment and into a social interaction, I'd obsessively think about every single thing I'd said throughout the night, wondering if I'd hurt anyone's feelings, or inadvertently caused them to hate me. I detested hugs, and physical interaction made my skin crawl.

As this spiral downward continued, it started affecting my health. I dropped 30lbs in a year, and the crushing anxiety caused daily bouts of diarrhea. It also helped destroy one relationship, and didn't help much in my next one. I'd leave restaurants in the middle of the meal because I was having an anxiety attack. I couldn't concentrate at work, and my job performance was suffering tremendously.

And still, I insisted it was somehow related to something physically wrong with me. I convinced myself I was lactose intolerant. I was sure I had celiac disease. Never once did I admit to myself that this was something entirely different.

I was 25 years old when all of this started. Seven years later, I decided to finally get to the root of the problem. I was about to be married in a year and I was determined to fix all of this before the wedding. It wasn't fair to my soon-to-be-wife (who, I will admit, was incredibly patient through all of these eccentricities and anxiety attacks.)

I went to my primary care physician and told him I'd had diarrhea almost constantly for the past seven years. He immediately scheduled me to see a proctologist who then signed me up for a colonoscopy. When those tests came back negative and there was nothing wrong with my GI tract, the proctologist pulled me into his office and had the exact conversation I should have had with myself seven years earlier.

This wasn't physical. This was mental. So, he put me on a low dosage of Lexapro - an antidepressant (note: I'm not now nor was I then depressed, but it helps with OCD and anxiety as well).

**My world fucking changed.**

On the day of my colonoscopy, I weighed 125lbs. Nine months later at my wedding, I was 160lbs. I became more physically active, joined a rowing program, and saw an increase in my social life. I was outgoing again. With less to worry about, I was free to think creatively again. And the only negative thought that remained was that I'd wasted seven whole years fighting this disease when it could have been rectified simply if I'd only have been honest with myself.

One year after my colonoscopy, my proctologist scheduled me for a follow-up visit. He was late coming into the room, and there was a somber mood throughout the office. When he did finally come in and ask me how things were going, I teared up. I thanked him for saving my life. I thanked him for giving me my life back. And I thanked him for taking the time to really figure out what was wrong, rather than just send me to another doctor. He teared up too. He told me it'd been a hard day, and that one of his patents had just died from colon cancer, but that this sort of success was what made his work worthwhile. And for the first time in my whole life, I hugged a doctor.

It's been five years since everything was "fixed." While I do have the occasional anxiety attack, they can be measured seasonally rather than daily. I'm never afraid to leave my house, and I look forward to social situations. I also only get diarrhea when I decide it's smart to eat three full bags of *Sour Patch Kids.* I'm still on Lexapro, and I meditate regularly to help keep me calm.

So, why tell you all this? I'm telling you this to tell you about this. To create a dialogue. To share my experience and provide proof that getting help works. These diseases thrive in the darkness, and no one should waste 7 days let alone 7 years in silence fighting them.

# Quit

## *Week Twelve*

The walls of the ice cave flickered with the dancing light of the fire. The team - arranged in a messy circle around the camp fire - took this moment to decompress from the day-long climb they'd just endured on the southern face of Gangkhar Puensum. So far, this covert mission had been successful, with minimal interference from the Bhutanese government or mother nature.

Harris glanced over the crew he'd assembled, and for the first time all day, cracked a smile. They were motley, rugged, and each had an over-sized personality, but they were some of the best mountain climbers he knew. And he saw the completion and subsequent rest from the first day's climb as a chance for them to get to know each other better.

Mark and Dill, friends since high school, were busy entertaining the rest of the group with a story from their past.

"...and Dill comes to my place with, like, three Thanksgiving-sized turkeys," Mark says, letting the image float in the silence, "and they're totally uncooked."

"Last time you told this, there were only two turkeys," Dill interjects.

"Whatever. Dill has more than one turkey."

"Lots of dead turkeys, got it," Devon says, hoping to move the story along.

"So I ask him what's up, and he tells me not to worry about it. But at this point, I'm fully invested. Motherfucker just shows up at my door with," Mark takes a moment to look at Dill, "*several* dead turkeys. I mean, this is not a normal occurrence."

"You're really going to tell the whole thing?" Dill asks.

"Now we're all invested," Harris states - his first words since putting his pack down.

"Right. So Dill has these birds, and at that point it'd been like, what? A day and a half since your last cigarette?"

"Something like that."

"And so Dill throws these things on my kitchen table and just goes at them with a knife. Starts cutting meat off of them."

A wave of realization passes over Devon's face.

"Yeah, uncooked poultry. He takes this shit and just starts pounding it into his mouth."

"How was I to know? I didn't take home economics."

"Jesus. How much did you eat?" Chris asks.

"Not that much, it was hard to get down."

"You are such an idiot."

"Hey man, I wanted to quit smoking."

"By going 'cold-turkey.' It's just an expression."

"Yeah. I get that now. And by the way, at any point you could have stopped me."

"No way. I felt like this was a teachable moment for you."

"So what happened? Did you quit smoking" Devon again tries to push the conversation.

"This?" Mark says through laughter, "This is the best part."

"I ate a shit load of raw turkey. Literally pounds of this stuff. I got salmonella poisoning real bad."

"Real bad." Mark punctuates.

"So I spend the next four days in bed, just puking and shitting, shitting and puking. I lost weight. I wanted to die. I couldn't move. And the thing is, I was sick for so long that my cigarette cravings stopped."

"Because," Devon says, "you quit cold turkey."

"Exactly! I haven't had a cigarette since!"

Harris laughs, "This is remarkable."

"No kidding," says Devon, "You should open a clinic."

"Oh, I've considered it. But I doubt I'd get past the FDA."

## Between Everything and Nothing

*Week Thirteen*

It was my *Rolling Stones* shirt that gave Emily a reason to talk to me. We were walking past each other just after fourth period when she pointed at the giant illustrated lips on my chest and said without an ounce of irony, "Nice shirt."

This first interaction lead to debates about who was the better guitarist, Clapton or Richards, during lunch, and long discussions about the best albums of the year while we sat on the hood of my dad's car in the parking lot after school.

The sun would begin to set, and I'd nervously try to think of another question to ask her, in the chance her answer might mean I'd get to spend a few more seconds with her. Before I went to sleep each night, I'd look at the short texts she'd sent me throughout the day, and mull over what she said, and if I could derive some sort of secret girl code out of them.

"You have to listen to Sam Cooke" could easily mean she wanted to date me. "Pretty sure I just failed that test" could be interpreted as her broadcasting her undying love for me. But because I'd never had a girlfriend before, I didn't know how to initiate that conversation with Emily. I just knew that whatever this was, I wanted more of it, more of her.

---

I'd seen him a dozen or so times, but I'd never spoken to him. I wasn't even entirely sure of his name. But I knew he seemed like the kind of guy who'd probably have some deep interests. An encyclopedic knowledge of foreign films, or a fascination with geography. His eyes were so intense and full of study that it seemed like he was always working things out. Like he'd seen the man behind the curtain and we were just too blind to see.

He existed in the shadows, a lack of confidence, or energy, or both, kept him from the center of things. Like most of the kids in my high school, when the final bell rang, and we left the building, he'd cease to be.

I'd never had anything against him; I just felt like we swam in different channels. He did his thing and I did mine. It was the rule of the high school jungle. And it was through no fault of either of ours that we stayed in our separate animal kingdoms. It was just the way the cosmic architecture predetermined how we existed.

---

When a bullet enters the human body, it first punctures the skin, snapping it and pulling some of it forward along its trajectory. Next, it drags the muscles, veins, and arteries, pulling them, twisting them, and turning them to dust. It snaps bones, it decimates organs, and if it passes through the body, it does all of this twice; the second time in reverse. Behind the bullet exists a vacuum that's a whirl of chaos. Flesh, bone, and blood swirl together in a mixture that's both horribly cold and frighteningly hot.

The police will explain how the guy whose name I don't remember sprayed his assault rifle in an upward movement as he rushed into my classroom. The force of the gun firing pulled it upwards. I was hit twice and immediately fell back in my chair. With a collapsed left lung, I gasped for air and felt my throat fill up with blood. Through the shots, I heard glass breaking, people screaming, and doors slamming. Someone pulled the fire alarm. I couldn't move, I could barely breathe, and I felt something warm growing under my back.

Staring up at the perforated ceiling of my classroom, all the sound seemed to fade away. The confusion aligned in a straight line. My fractured breathing drifted into nothing. Time slowed and I sat between everything and nothing. Pictures of me riding my first bike, eating my first ice cream cone, and smiling with my family fell like falling Polaroids in front of my eyes. And the last time my synapses fired, they carried one single thought: I hoped Emily was ok.

---

I would have liked to see Emily one last time. To tell her everything I felt. To look into her eyes and see her soul staring back at me. To thank her for pointing at my shirt. For choosing to spend this short time on the planet with me.

But as time goes on, I fear I'll forget pieces of Emily. The way the corner of her lips - right where they met her cheeks - formed a perfect angle. The way she took a deep breath right before launching into a sentence she knew would be long and detailed. How she could quote lyrics that were 50 years old, but couldn't quite memorize the steps for cell mitosis. How her smile meant the world to me.

Emily would go on. She'd take more breaths. My name would fade from the news footage and the papers, and it hurt to think that, for Emily, I'd one day be "this guy she knew." And after that, the only thing that will be left of me is a number. A statistic.

## The Morning Run

*Week Fourteen*

They first showed up in Union Square. Then Washington Square Park. They spread to Times Square and Central Park until you'd see them in almost every major subway station in the city. Officially, they were the "Observers of God," but everyone else called them the "Foldies" due to their ubiquitous purple blindfolds.

Along with their blindfolds, they wore earplugs all of the time and dressed in yellow. They never spoke. And if you touched one, they'd pull back and scream deathly wails. Friends would swear they'd actually spoke to one. Others would claim they'd seen them take their blindfolds off. But as the months went on and their numbers grew, no one knew anything for sure. Rumors and guesses swirled around the city about their origins. Where did they come from? Who lead them? Why did they attempt to cut themselves off - sensorially - in some of the busiest places in the city? And, like most of the off-beat characters in New York City, the more you looked into their past, the more complicated it became.

---

She never went looking for trouble. But she was so mad at the world, so ready for a fight, that if trouble came her way, she said: bring it on. Sarah had signed her divorce papers five months ago. Her ex had moved out a year earlier. And the young little thing he was currently living with was nothing more than an attempt to show the world that he liked pretty things.

So fuck him. Fuck her. And right now, fuck the world.

She didn't need any of it, didn't ask for any of it, and the one thing that she did want was to punch a motherfucker in the face. Hard.

So she did what she always did. She ran. Fast and long. Each step pushed off a piece of her world, and sent it flying behind her. It was therapy.

The path down the Henry Hudson was Sarah's favorite running route in the city. She could start at 96th Street and run practically uninterrupted for seven miles down to Battery Park, then hop on the 1 subway and be back home and ready for work in under two hours. Due to the nature of her job, she was often running alone or with "third shifters" who'd either just gotten off work or were about to head in throughout the early morning hours.

It was the perfect route that split the narrow ridge of land between the Westside and the Hudson River. She'd watch as the streetlights turned off, and as the early morning shadows shortened as the sun rose slowly over the city. And best of all, if she'd lucked out with timing, she could race barges being pushed down river.

For five years, she'd never had any issues. She'd get the occasional wolf whistle, or receive a lingering stare from someone running past her, but the can of mace she kept affixed to her running shorts kept anyone from trying something stupid. In the past, she'd flip them off or tell them some naughty things they could do to their mothers, but that just seemed to make them more interested.

On the colder mornings, a fog would form over the warmer waters of the river. And on this day, the fog was cotton-thick. Luckily, Sarah knew every crack, turn, and pothole on the path. She memorized the trees, she knew when there was new graffiti, and when something was out of place, she felt it.

And on this day, through the fog, something was definitely not right. She was on the section of the running path that separated from the land and ran over the water via a bridge for several hundred meters. The early morning light was muted through the fog, but she could sense there was something out there. Her hand instinctively fell to her can of mace, as she slowed to a walk. She removed her headphones and heard a strange gurgling sound. A wet rhythmic suction noise that sounded like canned cranberry juice falling out of its container.

She saw it hanging limply down - the long and now-unmistakable purple silk of one of the Foldies' blindfolds. Sarah followed it up with her eyes, and, through the fog, could just make out the circular monolith of an outflow pipe. A trickle of water poured out and into the Hudson through the grate of the pipe. And on the other side of the grate, through the tangled mass of a torn yellow dress, was the pale, contorted, motionless face of a woman.

Sarah jumped back in shock and almost lost her footing. She turned her head half out of horror, and half out of respect for what once was this person. She pulled her armband off her left shoulder, and with shaky hands, pulled out her phone. Immediately, she dialed 911 and reported the body.

She could hear sirens start up from somewhere deep in the concrete canyons, and grew anxious knowing she had to spend the next few minutes alone with the body as it sloshed around with the current making its way out of the grate of the outflow pipe.

Trouble had found her.

## In the Forgotten Season, Chapter Two

### *Week Fifteen*

The main reason people travel to Sudbury, Ontario – and let me be perfectly clear here, there's no reason for anyone to travel to Sudbury, Ontario – is to watch industrial rail cars dump molten slag down hills of black ash at night. The second reason to travel to Sudbury, Ontario is to see what was once the tallest freestanding smokestack in the world. The plumes of grey smoke that escaped from this Empire State Building-sized chimney produced acid rain far and wide across eastern Canada and the United States.

At the turn of the century, the discovery of nickel deposits in and around Sudbury resulted in the establishment of large-scale mining operations in the area. This caused an almost total loss of native-vegetation throughout the city, and the industries that popped up blackened the newly exposed rock formations with soot. If you're seeking out Hell on Earth, one need not look farther than the charred landscape of Sudbury, Ontario.

In 1989, my parents took us to Sudbury for our family summer vacation.

With a few stops on either side, our family piled into my mother's Peugeot and drove up to see Canada's industrial wasteland firsthand. Other families went to Cape Cod, the Outerbanks, or Maine, but the Uhrynowski family needed to experience the fun and lung cancer cough-inducing side of Canada's 24th largest city.

Our car trips always had a few prerequisites. Most importantly, Eric and I were not to cross the taped-off centerline of the car. I sat on the left, and

Eric on the right. We'd fold down the armrest in the middle to ensure stray fists, boogers, or spit didn't cross the threshold. Second, Eric insisted on listening, on eternal repeat, to *Genesis'* crowning achievement in album creation, *Invisible Touch*. Third, we didn't eat at rest stops. Individual ham and cheese sandwiches were made days before, placed in a cooler in the trunk, and handed out only when we stopped for gas. With those key items in place, we were free to get underway.

"She does a handstand an invisible touch it. She thinks she's eaten and grabs right hold of your heart."

"Those aren't the lyrics," Eric says an hour into our trip.

"I'm pretty sure that's what he's saying," I respond without an ounce of confidence.

"Phil Collins is singing about handstands?"

"Yeah, he even says 'she has a built-in ability' which is all about her gymnastic skills."

"You're wrong."

"No, you're wrong."

"So, what are the lyrics then?"

"I don't know, but I'm sure it's not about handstands."

"Bite me."

I get a look from my father in the rear-view mirror. Eric, out of sight of my parents, gives me the finger and laughs.

"Mom, Eric just gave me the finger!"

"Which one," she says still reading her magazine from the passenger seat.

"The bad one," I say, "The REALLY bad one."

"Did not," Eric says, sticking out his tongue, "You're a liar."

"Oh yeah? How about this." And I reach across the DMZ, grab Eric's still-extended finger, and bend it backwards. He screams like I just stabbed him in the heart.

"Hey, you two, quit it," the magazine falls into my mom's lap as she turns around with ignited eyes. "Adam, get on the other side of the line. Eric, stop giving your brother the finger."

"Fine. Can you turn it up?" he says, "I don't want to hear Adam singing the wrong words. Besides he sings like a girl."

"Eric, be nice."

Be nice? Be nice! With adrenalin pumping through my brain, everything slowed down. My head turned to the right, with the bones cracking in rhythm. I caught a glint of light off Eric's eyes as they turned toward mine. I realized what I was about to do was dangerous. It won't end well. But he drew first blood, and I needed to establish dominance in the backseat of this car. I needed to set the tone for the rest of the trip. I held up not one, but two fists, both clenched tightly. Slowly, deliberately, the middle fingers on both hands began to raise and I bit my lower lip in anger.

Eric's mouth dropped open with incredulity. He pulled his arm back, smiled briefly, made a first, and punched me in the throat.

I felt the tears first. The shock of what just happened took seconds to calculate inside my brain, but my go-to-emotional defense system kicked in from the microsecond his hand made contact with my neck. I noticed the smile on Eric's face which only added to the tears. From somewhere off in the distance, my mother's voice sliced through the air and landed in our ears like a hawk descending upon two helpless salamanders.

"Do you even want to go on this trip!? We can turn this car around right now if you two don't shape up." The idea of not seeing glorious downtown Sudbury was, for a fleeting second, an actually possibility. For a brief second, the question hits home: do I even want to go on this trip?

"Eric, the tape is getting turned off. Adam, stop crying. We're driving in silence for the next hour."

"But he started it," I pleaded.

"It doesn't matter who started it, it matters who finished it," and with that, my mom reminded us of a basic rule of fighting in the Uhrynowski family. All would be okay as long as you were the one to finish it.

"So I finished it, right mom? Because I hit him last?" Eric said, still smiling.

"No, I finished it because I didn't hit you back," I snapped back with an air of condescension, my tears quickly drying up.

"Both of you, be quiet. One hour."

"Listen to your mother," my father said, putting a death knell into the battle.

---

"You need to watch out. You're probably going to be an alcoholic," my mom said, flicking her cigarette ash into the ashtray in front of us. We were halfway between Niagara Falls and Sudbury at a roadside restaurant that more than likely had "shack" or "family" or "backyard" in the name, enjoying – for once – non-ham and cheese sandwiches.

"Why am I going to be an alcoholic?" I asked, not fully understanding who or what an alcoholic is.

"Because you have a small upper lip. People with small upper lips tend to become alcoholics."

Eric laughed and pointed at me.

"Wait, is this true?" I asked with a relative amount of concern.

"Yes. Look at your grandmother. Small upper lip, loves vodka," and she was right, my grandmother did have a small upper lip and she could definitely drink a vodka or nine.

My mother stubbed out her cigarette, its dying streams of smoke puttering out in the cool Ontario air. "It's why I don't drink. I don't want to risk it. That sort of thing can really do damage to you and to your family."

"So what should I do?" I asked, "Is there medicine for it?"

"No. You should never drink alcohol. Ever."

This was the sort of scientific fact my mother was famous for stating. An often-misheard statement that she sold as fact. And it worked, for the most part. I didn't touch alcohol throughout high school and most of college. I did, however, start drinking in my 20's and have yet to develop anything close to bordering on an addiction.

"What about me?" Eric chimed in, "Am I going to be an alcoholic?"

"No, you'll probably develop diabetes."

---

"I don't know, it just got stuck," I said, "like I closed it and it won't open back up," we'd made it to Sudbury and things were not going well.

"Did you jiggle it, Peter?" which was my mom's solution for everything.

"Yes Dane, I jiggled it. It won't budge," my dad was clearly reaching the end of his rope and we were only a few days into this trip.

"Well, what's in there? Just our suitcases?"

"Nice going, Adam," Eric was quick to identify blame.

"OK, let's figure this out. When Adam closed the trunk it somehow locked. The key won't open it, and there's no access to the trunk via the backseat. Maybe we can use the automatic car locks?" my dad was stepping in with his even-tempered logic.

The main problem, aside from having zero access to our clothes, toiletries, and ham sandwiches, was that my parents had purchased a Peugeot – a notoriously shitty French car. Somehow, the lock cylinder failed when it slammed shut, resulting in a solidly secured trunk.

Attempts at using the automatic locks failed to rectify the situation. The Uhrynowski family, in a stale hotel parking lot, had no (fresh) clothes.

Off in the distance, the Sudbury smokestack puffed more soot into the air, creating a line of smog across the horizon. All four of us sat on a curb, watching the smoke travel across the sky in silence. My mother was frustrated. My dad was organizing potential solutions in his head. Eric blamed me. I ran over how and why it happened again and again in my head.

"Screw it. Let's go to K-Mart," my mom stood up, stubbed her burning cigarette out on the ground, and hopped in the passenger seat. I'd never been to a K-Mart. In fact, the term "K-Mart" was only mentioned in our suburban Connecticut family when we were describing something or someone of poor-quality. For example:

"This garden hose has a hole in it already, it's totally K-Mart," or, "He uses words like 'ain't' and 'y'all.' He's K-Mart." I'm not proud of this. I'm sure my father cringed every time we said it. But it had entered and found a nice home in the vernacular of the Uhrynowski family.

But actually going into a K-Mart? Actually creating an informed opinion of the store and clientele we'd poked fun at all these years? This would be a first. And so, we piled into our disastrously built French sardine can on wheels with a locked trunk and found the closest Canadian K-Mart.

My mom grabbed three pairs of t-shirts, three pairs of socks, three pairs of underwear, and three pairs of shorts for each of us. The entire time, she held her head high and said not a word. We might not have our actual clothes, but we were going to maintain our dignity, even if that meant wearing knock-off clothing brands and polyester underpants.

That night, we drove out to the mining section just north of town. Still reeling from my mistake earlier, I figured this would be a good place for them to dump my body. Instead, we sat on the roof of the Peugeot and watched as a train slowly pulled up on the top of a low black ridge. One-by-one, the train cars - shaped like giant metal bowls - tipped over, pouring their bright red molten slag down on the heaps of black. As it flowed out, splashing down the side of the hill and sending sparks scattering into the wind, I looked at the faces of my family in their already-fraying new clothes. With their eyes glowing with wonder (or, let's be honest, the burning remnants of smelting waste), smiles slowly rose on their faces. We'd come a long way to witness this moment, and we earned every second of it.

## Haven, Part I

*Week Sixteen*

"This is not going to go well," thought Cooper, carefully stepping over a fallen tree branch. His hands dripped with sweat - even in the dead of night, the air was thick with humidity. It'd been a few hours since he'd heard the dogs, and the full moon gave him just enough light to push the dogs and their masters behind him.

Throughout his short journey, he'd seen faces everywhere. In the limbs of trees. In patterns on the ground. And in the shadows of his periphery. Even this far into the woods, he felt like he was being watched. He called them the *fatalwoyi*, a name that traced its lineage to that land across the sea. Many had claimed to see the *fatalwoyi* sitting menacingly in the rigging of the slavers' ships, floating above the fields of cotton, or as phantoms crawling through the dark woods. Cooper felt like their bony claws were tracing over his body, just waiting to catch him off guard. And it was that feeling that propelled him forward.

Cooper vaguely knew the direction he was heading in. Rumors had spread throughout the South about these camps - small free settlements in hard-to-reach areas that were populated by escaped slaves. Old Joe, the plantation's oldest slave, claimed to have actually been to one years ago, long before the war. The thought of freedom sparked hope in Cooper, and he listened to Joe's every word, dreaming of the day he'd step into just such a village. Joe taught him to look for the signs and symbols, how the tides worked, and the best way to travel safely without fear of discovery.

On the night Cooper prepared to leave, Old Joe - who'd outright refused to accompany Cooper on his journey due to his age - created a perfect, surprising, and devastating distraction that gave Cooper just enough time to escape. Cooper's tears soaked through his eye lids as he hugged the dying man. And with strained breath and voice, Old Joe pulled him in and spoke one simple word into his ear, "run."

He never looked back. Cooper made a beeline through the fields toward a row of trees that stood at the far end of the property and dissolved into the lowlands beyond. Once there, he ran down the dirt road away from Eden Fields, away from town, and toward freedom.

Cooper only travelled at night and followed the murky waters of the inlets that sliced into the South Carolina Coast. Small piles of stones and sticks arranged in unique patterns were telltale signs left years before by fellow runaways letting Cooper know he was headed in the right direction. If he'd planned well enough, he'd make it to Moreland in a few days.

The camp of Moreland was established along a tributary of the May River a few miles north of Savannah. After the Union freed what was then known as the "Sea Islands," and the white population fled, this section of South Carolina was given to the freemen in what became the Port Royal Experiment. Moreland, situated on the southern reaches of the Sea Islands, focused more on fishing than the farming that was done inland, and because it was swampy and hidden, it was perfect for a small group of people looking to find peace. Cooper didn't care what the conditions were like at the camp, the only way he'd return to Eden Fields was as a corpse.

The moonlight was dulled beneath the Spanish moss that clung to the oak where Cooper had stopped to rest. He used a rock to break open a few chestnuts he'd collected throughout the night, and complemented those with a handful of partridge berries he'd pulled from a bush nearby. While it wasn't a feast by any stretch of the imagination, if this is what freedom tasted like, he'd take it.

He let out a deep breath. A mixture of relief and exhaustion.

And still, the *fatalwoyi* persisted. Noises far in the distance. Movements in the underbrush. Unexplainable lights that dashed over the treetops and sent his heart racing. Cooper's respite was short lived. A snapping stick a few feet from him sent him running. His ragged shirt flapped behind him, and the forest blurred into a deep indigo as he sprinted forward.

The forest floor seemed to float below his feet as his fear propelled him forward into the darkness. The *fatalwoyi*, the plantation owners, the dogs, or whatever other evils pursued him would never catch him.

His toes dug under the root of a tree, sending Cooper flying forward into the dirt. His face pressed into the ground, he couldn't detect the presence in front of him. Slowly lifting his head, he traced the two feet up the body and into the face of what could best be described as a woman both human and not. Eyes with no pupils. Hair that flowed despite the lack of a breeze. And skin that seemed to suck in any and all light in the vicinity. He went to scream, but the apparition raised a long bony finger to her mouth and exhaled with a guttural "shhhh."

Cooper couldn't tell if he were paralyzed due to fear, or if this *fatalwa* was actually keeping him from moving. In the distance, he could see the flicker of torches; no doubt the same group of men who'd been tracking him since he left Eden Fields. In a last ditch effort, he grabbed a rock and hurled it at the *fatalwa*, but instead of knocking her back, the stone *went through her*.

At this, the *fatalwa* looked down at Cooper with her dead white eyes. Her mouth opened larger than humanly possible revealing a black nothingness inside. The scream that escaped from the giant maw was hideously loud, and, to Cooper, filled with all the sounds he'd ever heard in his life coming out as one chaotic mass. And despite the sonic blast escaping the *fatalwa*, Cooper found himself being pulled toward her. He grabbed for purchase in the dirt, but the mouth continued to grow larger and larger until finally, as Cooper fell into the abyss of the vacuum, he found all of his senses turning out like separate candle flames extinguishing in the night.

---

"Hey," the voice said, followed by a gentle shake of the shoulder, "Hey you. Who are you?"

Cooper slowly opened his eyes and the bright light of the sun hit his pupils and shrunk them to the size of a pin head.

"I said, who are you?" repeated the voice, "what's your name?"

The world came into focus, and Cooper found himself in the same low country forest he'd been in last night. He quickly started and looked around nervously for any sign of the *fatalwa*.

"It's okay, son" said the man, "you're home."

"Home?" Thought Cooper, confused and still trying to get his bearings. "Yes. Welcome to Moreland."

## Love Actually: Redux

### *Week Seventeen*

INT. PETER AND JULIET'S FOYER - NIGHT

PETER opens the door and sees MARK standing in his front doorway holding a BOOMBOX and a series of CUE cards. PETER is pleased to see MARK and smiles. MARK, not expecting PETER to answer the door, is taken a back, flummoxed, and is unsure how to proceed. Of course, he doesn't want to tell his best friend that he's in love with his wife.

PETER

Hi!

MARK holds up his finger as if to say 'be quiet.' We quickly cut to JULIET on the couch watching television.

JULIET

Who is it?

Back on MARK, he rolls his eyes, upset that the love of his life is mere footsteps away and this has gone so wrong. He hesitantly shows PETER the card that reads "Say It's Carol Singers."

PETER

(Intrigued, but confused)

It's uh, carol singers.

In the living room, JULIET grabs the TV REMOTE and is waiting for PETER to return.

JULIET

Give them a quid and tell them to bugger off.

MARK presses play on the BOOMBOX and "Silent Night" begins to play softly. He goes through the cue cards, all the while intending them for JULIET. However, PETER misunderstands the meaning behind them and assumes that MARK is professing his love for him. Finally, the cue cards end on "Merry Christmas" and PETER mouths "Merry Christmas" to MARK. MARK, still unsure of what just happened and how he could have calculated this so poorly, holds his two thumbs up hesitantly. MARK then walks away.

EXT. LONDON STREET - NIGHT

MARK is walking down the street holding his CUE CARDS while his BOOMBOX still plays "Silent Night." In the distance, we see PETER run toward him. Now face to face, PETER kisses MARK and looks in his eyes.

We are then taken through a quick series of scenes, each with PETER and MARK becoming noticeably older.

We are in a LAWYER's office with JULIET crying on one side of a table, while PETER holds MARK's hand. MARK is still absolutely shocked.

We are at the wedding of PETER and MARK. PETER is overjoyed, but MARK maintains his shocked expression.

We see PETER and MARK meeting their adopted ASIAN child for the first time. PETER gives the child a huge hug. MARK remains motionless and shocked.

Next, we see PETER and MARK dropping off their fully-grown CHILD at UNIVERSITY. PETER wipes away a tear. MARK is still shocked.

Finally, we're in a HOSPITAL as MARK holds PETER'S hand as he lays dying in a HOSPITAL BED. The EKG readout falls to a flatline, and PETER'S head falls on the pillow. He is dead. MARK places PETER'S hand at his side and walks out of the room.

We focus on MARK.

MARK

Enough. Enough now.

FADE OUT

# Death by Misadventure

## *Week Eighteen*

If you'd have been on the water that day, you would have heard it before you saw it. Laughter dancing across the dark and still waters of the harbor. The fog was thick but bright - a white wall of mist that seemed to magnify the sun above. And inside it, the laughter. Strained, faded, but joyous.

If you'd have been on the water that day, you would have seen him appear. A man as knotted and worn as the wooden boat he rowed. The curtain of the fog lifted slightly around him as he passed through. Each stroke of the oar sent his small craft lurching deeper and deeper into the unknown boundaries of the harbor. Each stroke in rhythm with his laughter.

If you'd have been on the water that day, you would have smelled the paradoxical welcoming rot of low tide. An odor both foul and, for those who spent their days around the harbor, assuring. The tide would rise twice a day. The tide would fall twice a day. And that cadence and the accompanying smell reminded the dock workers, the fisherman, and the sailors that the world was still spinning.

And there, deep now inside the fog, the old man stopped rowing letting his craft drift slowly to the exact spot he intended. The old man stopped laughing. He peered over the gunwale into the water, gently tilting his rowboat to one side, and looking down his reflection made him smile.

He reached below his seat, and grasped with knobby fingers, a metal ring holding three old, rusted, and distinct skeleton keys. His hands shook as he raised them, and the jangle of them bouncing off one another sent a clang piercing through the fog. He peered over the side once more, sure now that he'd found the exact spot. And without celebration or fanfare, he dropped the keys into the water and watched them sink until they could no longer be seen.

His laughter returned. Placing his oars back in the oarlocks, he began to row.

If you'd have been on the water that day, you would have caught the last sight of the man, smiling, laughing, and disappearing forever inside the harbor fog.

## Commercial Break

*Week Nineteen*

Instinctively, I look down at my hands - a slight cold wetness forms in the creases of my palms - and I twist the empty skin of my left ring finger. The studio lights are bright, and I'm sure if someone were to stand behind me, the lights would illuminate my inner organs like a macabre shadow puppet play centered around an overheating heart.

A production assistant has just informed me that we'll be resuming taping in a few minutes. Behind the wall to my right is my girlfriend, and over the next few hours, I will attempt to win back her love from the other two contestants.

Bachelor One is the guy she went to college with and recently met up with again during a trip to California. They quickly rekindled a romance and, as he informed me before the taping, spent most of the night looking for an empty space to "fuck in." He's the type of guy who winks when he talks about a woman's personality, and proudly and erroneously "rounds up" when counting off the women he's slept with.

Bachelorette Two looks peculiarly like my girlfriend. Her long brown hair with hints of auburn streaked throughout cascade down her shoulders and back. She stands a little taller than my girlfriend. She's more assured and more proud. She seems like the type of person who could use big words like "zeitgeist" and "parsimonious" correctly and confidently in a sentence. She's the ideal, or, more correctly, my girlfriend's idea of the ideal.

I'm Bachelor Three, still unsure of how I got here and wondering when and why I signed up for this. There'd been some bumps - arguments, disagreements, and an instance of cheating - but all of these were dulled by my genuine love for her. That didn't seem to matter. Because I was now on national television hoping my answers to her pre-written questions would be enough to win her back.

A person with a headset counts down from five behind a camera and points at the host. The host welcomes everyone back from the commercial break and reminds us that my girlfriend behind the wall has some hard choices to make. His billboard of white teeth clack into smile at the end of each sentence because no matter how this ends up - he's still getting paid.

I hear her clear her throat - the studio mics pick up any and all hiccups, snorts, and laughs. I wonder if it can hear my heart beating. The same voice that cried when she told me she loved me asks, "Bachelorette Two, do you believe in love at first sight?"

"Absolutely not. Love is something that's built, it's not just some random thing you happen upon," Bachelorette Two pauses and thinks for a second, "But you know what, you can love yourself at first sight."

"Interesting. Bachelor One, same question."

"Baby, once you get on the other side of this wall and see me, you'll know for a fact that love at first sight exists."

"Wow. Ok. And Bachelor Three...?"

---

I'd been at work late, and the subways were backed up. The 2nd Avenue Subway was still years away from being completed, so the Lexington Line was - typically - notoriously overcrowded. I reached the fifth floor of my apartment building, fumbled for my keys, and pushed my way into my front door with an exasperated breath. In the distance, I heard my roommate talking to someone.

I rolled my eyes, wanting only some relaxation in front of the television. This stranger would undoubtedly cut into my attempt at eating a horribly constructed dinner, drinking cheap beer, and passing out in front of some shitty reality programming.

I slogged off my coat, and tucked my bag into my room, then trudged out into the living room to see who this interloper was.

My roommate introduced us, but I don't remember saying hello. I don't remember telling her my name. I just remember thinking, "This girl is going to be so much trouble."

My roommate fell into the distance, swallowed by a room that no longer needed her there. She may have gone to get food. She may have lit the apartment on fire. There was a connection happening in that small living room and she wasn't part of it.

We spoke all night. And for the next week, everything was brighter, more colorful, and this wonderful person who I'd known for only a few short days had made me rethink all that was possible in life.

---

"Love at first sight is real. Absolutely." I say, my first confident statement of the program.

"Ok, a man who thinks true love is a reality," the host smirks into the camera, "how cute."

"Uh, I have a follow-up," my girlfriend asks from her corner of the studio, "Bachelor Three, where would we go on our first date?"

---

"No one wants me here. I'm going to go." she says not as a threat but as a resignation.

"Well, I don't care about them. I want you here. And if you're leaving, I'm leaving too," I respond with an unexpected coolness. She grabs my hand and we run out of the bar into the rush of cold wind blowing through the wide avenues of the Upper East Side.

Once we caught our breath from climbing the five flights of stairs to the railroad apartment I shared with her best friend, things went from flirtatious tension to parental advisory. And even though she left to go to work the next morning, I crawled back into bed and hugged my pillows trying to relive the magic of the night before over and over in my head.

---

The host cuts in, "Bachelor Three? We're waiting."

"Uh, we'd grab some drinks with friends. Then head back to my apartment for a nightcap." I keep it clean for the television viewing audience.

The host continues and moves through my competition. Bachelor One invents some wonderful - though absurdist - date involving horseback riding on a beach and drinking margaritas on a boat. The fool doesn't even know she hates tequila. Bachelorette Two talks about discovering themselves. Understanding what it is that they want together, and how best to reach their goals. This response gets a positive reaction from my girlfriend.

"Bachelor One, what are your best qualities?" she asks by reading off a blue notecard in front of her. Bachelor One shifts in his chair and smirks bordering on a smile.

"That's a great question. I'd have to say that I'm exciting. I'm different. And I'll challenge you."

"Bachelorette Two, same question."

"I'm driven. I'm successful. And most importantly, I won't let anything stand in my way of happiness."

Subconsciously, I lean away from Bachelorette Two.

"And finally, Bachelor Three, how would you answer that question?"

---

We are on a hammock just after sunset. The summer birds have gone to sleep, and fireflies blink all around us. This is the first moment we've had alone all weekend. Her head is on my chest, and I feel a small warm wet spot form on my shirt near her eye. I pull her in tightly silently letting her know that I know. She looks up at me, smiles, and buries her face deeper into the comfort of my chest.

---

"I'm a good listener," I respond, sure that I've said the wrong thing.

The host cringes a bit.

"OK!" the host with the teeth again, "Here's our last round of questions. Then we'll see if we've made a match here tonight!"

Behind the wall, my girlfriend's chair squeaks as she turns in it. I imagine her biting her bottom lip as she did so often when she was troubled or deep in thought.

"Bachelor Two," she says, "If I had to end our relationship to figure out who I was, would you let me go?"

Bachelorette Two seems taken aback by the question. She thinks for a second and finally leans into the mic, "Well, yes. But I'm hoping that we could find each other together."

Bachelor One doesn't even wait for her to repeat the question, "No way! You'd never leave me. I'm all you need and all you want."

"Bachelor Three," she pauses briefly, "Bachelor Three, if I had to leave you to figure out who I was, would you let me go?

---

She's been gone for a week. I'm still finding her bobby pins everywhere, and the perfume I bought her for her birthday a few years ago still lingers on the pillows. Our apartment is lonely, quiet, and different.

She'd taken a job out in California - one that seemed promising and exciting, and if I'm being totally honest, a needed change. Her infidelity a few months back was really nothing more than a "par for the course" of a relationship in turmoil. Before that, she'd started taking weekend trips without me, and I'd stay out late at bars with friends, trying to think up excuses not to come home early. We were growing distant, two large masses feeding off each other's gravitational pull but needing to explore the "what ifs" of an endless universe.

When she told me she wanted to take the job, I knew there was no convincing her otherwise. Her eyes had a flame in them - one that I hadn't seen in months. And so, I said I'd support her no matter what.

---

"Of course," I mutter into the microphone, "if you haven't found yourself, I wouldn't want to keep you from figuring that out."

It's a lie. I wanted her to go, but more than anything, I wanted her to go and realize she needed me. To realize that I needed her. To come back because we needed us.

I slumped in my chair, tired, worn out, and defeated. I knew how this was going to play out even before I entered the studio this morning.

"Alright folks, let's see who she's picked."

"I've given it careful consideration, and I think I'm most compatible with Bachelorette Two."

Bachelorette Two stands up, the stage lights point toward her in unison bringing much needed darkness and letting my pupils expand for the first time in a few hours. She's laughing and covering her mouth like she just won an Oscar. The host guides her across the studio floor and behind the wall where my girlfriend - sorry, my ex-girlfriend - and Bachelorette Two undoubtedly embrace.

I don't bother seeing what the consolation prize is. I walk through the dark door to the studio, and out into world alone.

---

I roll over in what was once our bed in the boxed-up space that was once our apartment, and bury my face into what were once our pillows. And for the last few moments in this place we once called home, I replay only the good moments we shared together, thankful that we got to share them at all.

## Slide

*Week Twenty*

The pirate outfit was entirely unnecessary, but it made Digby Marks laugh. Procured from a custom shop in Denver, he'd taken the extra step of adding a parrot, formerly alive, currently taxidermized, and attaching it to the silk left shoulder of the billowy shirt. In his pockets, he kept a few fake, though heavy, Spanish doubloons. And as he looked out over the white peaks edging the Foxraven Valley, he often imagined they were gargantuan waves, ready to splinter his ship.

The previous night's snowfall had left little doubt on Digby Marks that today would be an ideal day to head back to his perch on Hawthorne Pass overlooking the back bowls of Foxraven Valley. Anyone who knows anything about mountain engineering will tell you that slopes angled between 25 degrees and 45 degrees fell into the slide zone. Two shallow to let snow buildup just runoff easily, and too steep to keep it from avalanching down once provoked. The mountain sides of the Foxraven Valley ranged from 32.3 degrees and 40.7 degrees, and the freshly fallen snow that sat on them was ready - no, *wanted* - to move.

Enter the Howitzer.

Lately, this particular cannon had been used to blow limbs and lives away in several Eastern Bloc countries. It's low velocity, but intimidating range, made it perfect for killing the proletariat from the comfort and safety of one's backyard. End an uprising while sipping on your morning coffee. Marks had purchased it, piece by piece, by a three-fingered arms dealer, and reassembled it in his garage. He then towed it - in the open and without cover - to Hawthorne Pass, deep in Foxraven Valley without incident or alarm.

The shells were bought from the back room of a military supply store. Surrounded by sniper flares, motion sensing trigger bombs, phase shifting alpha repeaters, 3D printable missile launcher blueprints, and remote controlled ballistic vests, 3 perfectly good and ready to use Howitzer shells were bought for less than a meal at one of those fancy restaurants that lined Pearl Street in Boulder.

The intent was never to kill. Marks didn't want a record. But what he did want was to, in his words, scare the fucking piss out of some rich city-dwelling assholes. And what better place to find rich city-dwelling assholes than at the Foxraven Ski Resort which just so happened to offer the chance for rich city-dwelling assholes to ride to the top of Foxraven Peak in a heated six-person Gondola for the low, low price of $120/day?

It was early. The lifts had only been spinning for a half an hour. It'd take a few more minutes for the pseudo-daredevils to head to the back bowls, hungry to try some of that "sweet pow" and make "first tracks." Before they arrived, Marks lined up his shot. Wind calculations were determined. Earth curvatures were estimated.

Through his binoculars, he watch two ski patrol members, make their way down the bowl, safely determining that their precious customers would be able to spend the day enjoying the wilderness and return to pay $120 the next day and do it all over again.

Finally, what looked like five guys in their late 20s and early 30s started down. Outfitted with horribly expensive rare-duck down feathered ski jackets, the latest titanium plated vacuum pocketed boots, and goggles tinted to reveal every edge line on the mountain, these were the targets.

Marks lit the fuse and ran back a few feet - the doubloons clanging in his pockets. THWUMP. The shell volleyed out of the Howitzer and began its journey to the pristine snow facade of Foxraven Ski Resort's second most-famous ski trail. (The first, known as *Doc's Knob,* was famous - or infamous - for being the location of a prominent American family's ill-fated capture the flag meets paintball meets skiing game in which an uncle wound up castrated by a low-hanging tree branch.)

Marks saw the cloud of snow rise up before he heard the report. The skiers, too dialed into the music blaring in their headphones and lost in their own self-importance, never heard the impact. In fact, they didn't even notice the slide for the first several hundred meters of its journey.

The avalanche sent a horizontal crack across the ridge line, and then spiderwebbed throughout sending the harder top layer of snow falling in sheets of incongruous polygons. Beneath those, the fine white powder acted as a liquid - molecules joining together in one common goal: reach the bottom of the mountain as quickly and with the most destruction as possible.

If Marks had timed it right - and it appeared as though he had - the slide would cross the skiers' paths within a dozen feet or so. Not enough to do any real damage, but enough to give them a story to share on their Facebook pages, Instagram photos, Snapstories, Yelp reviews, Strava feeds, Twitter accounts, and favorite obscure subreddits.

The first skier stopped. Without thinking, he snapped out of his skis, and began clump-running in his ski boots up the trail and away from the avalanche. The second, thinking it was a game, also took off his skis and attempted to race the first skier to an as-yet-undetermined finish line. The third, stopped and stared like a cupcake-deprived child at a birthday party as the wall of billowing snow crashed a few feet in front of him. The fourth, in fright, lost all bladder control, while skidding to a stop. The fifth. Well, the fifth went right into the slide.

Despite having a powerful military-grade weapon, an unpredictable form of nature, and a seething anger for well-to-do's, Marks had no intent on injuring or killing anyone today. And with the introduction of the fifth skier to the avalanche, this was going off script.

The rest of the group, skiers one and two having ended their race in a tie, watched hazily through the kicked-up snow cloud as the avalanche stopped. Marks tried desperately to figure out what had become of the fifth skier through his binoculars, but could only see the cumulus of snow boiling from the valley below.

Had Marks subscribed to *SkiGod69* on Instagram, he would have seen first-person footage - filmed in 4k resolution - of *SkiGod69* entering and seemingly surfing an avalanche for a few hundred meters before wrapping his body in the pointed canopy of an Aspen. It gained views exponentially once internet famous accounts like *SunsOutGunsOut* and *GaryAndBroseph* reposted it.

Five broken bones, a punctured lung, two missing teeth, and 33 seconds of internet gold brought caffeine-infused liquor companies, neon-named pain killer suppliers, and a t-shirt manufacturer who specialized in parodies of famous brand logos to *SkiGod69*'s hospital bed, all seeking to get in on the remaining 14:27 seconds of *SkiGod69*'s fame.

Marks did what any sane person in a pirate outfit with a stuffed parrot standing in the Colorado wilderness in the middle of winter would do, he pushed the Howitzer down the Hawthorne pass to hide the evidence, watching as the cannon picked up speed and tumbled loudly, end over end, before its barrel twisted itself around a series of loose boulders.

Above Hawthorne Pass in Foxraven Valley, above a strange man wearing a stuffed bird on his shoulder, a clump of freshly-fallen snow heard the thunderous clang of the Howitzer as it hit the rocks. And it knew its time for action had come.

## All At Sea

### *Week Twenty One*

Eric sits on his board, holds his sunburnt hand to his forehead in a salute, and looks out toward the horizon.

"Nothing coming," he says.

"Wind died down. Might be the end of the swells today," I respond in an attempt to use my best 'surfer' lingo.

Our boards bob over the shallow ocean waves, and we turn back to the beach and instinctively let the mild surf push us back toward shore. Dad is there to greet us, asks us how our rides were, and suggests coming back early tomorrow when the winds might pick up a bit. We grab our gear off the beach, feel the crust of drying salt water begin to form on our arms and legs, and head toward the house nestled in the dunes.

It had been firmly established that our family would vacation on the Outerbanks for two weeks each summer. It was no longer a question of where we were going, but when. Over the years, we watched as small beach huts were transformed to mansions on stilts. We saw dunes removed to make way for housing developments. And with the closest grocery store just a five minute drive down the road - a nice change from the 45 minute drive we used to have - we saw society creeping in on this small section of secluded paradise.

We didn't set out to be a surfing family. Coming from Connecticut and the flat expanse of Long Island Sound, we were better prepared to be a family who sailed, played golf, or went horseback riding. But once we caught sight of the double surf break off Currituck Beach in Corolla, all four of us knew what our collective family goal would be.

Cheap foam boogie boards gave way to slick-bottom boogie boards. From there, the roof rack on our family's car began sporting longboards, shortboards, and everything in between as we made the 12 hour trip down the east coast to North Carolina.

The days were spent in the waves, and our nights were spent feeling the rise and fall of the sea that'd been imprinted on our inner-ears all day long. But truly, what made these halcyon days so incredible wasn't the ocean. It wasn't the sun. It was that we were out there as family. My brother, my father, me, and, although she didn't surf, my mom who would swim out to the surf break and watch as we caught wave after wave.

While perched on our boards, we congratulated each other on rides. We spoke mythically about that one wave we took, or that one wave we missed. We remarked excitedly as dolphin traced parabolas in the distance. And when a swell would come in, all talk would cease as our family had one single goal: catch the biggest wave and ride it over the double break onto the beach.

We weren't a family that spent their summers poolside at a country club. We weren't a family that traveled from state to state singing in a band together. We were a family, that for two weeks every summer, surfed.

# Submerged

## *Week Twenty Two*

When the water gets low, the spire of the church pokes out. A few hundred yards to the south, the smokestacks of the old forge begin to show. The crumbling roads that once led into the old valley wander off into the abyss. The foundations of the small town crumble under the weight of the water, and deep in the murky darkness of the reservoir, a secret's heart still beats.

Every map you see today lists the area as the *Saugatuck Reservoir,* created by a dam that held back the water's namesake river in 1938. It provides water to some of the most affluent towns in Connecticut, but below it's surface rests a story washed away through time.

The villages of Hull and Valley Forge were, even by 1930s America standards, poor. But the people who lived in this peaceful valley in southern Connecticut were proud - especially when it came to the forge that helped produce steel used by the North during the Civil War. But the valley had something much more important than ore deposits. The valley had space. Specifically, space that resided in a river valley. And that's when the Bridgeport Hydraulic Company came knocking.

Through eminent domain, the BHC attempted to purchase the land rights to these villages just as they had for the land of the seven other reservoirs in the region. But Valley Forge and Hull were different. Because they were not as affluent, they could offer them pennies on the dollar for their land.

It's not like the residents had a choice.

During this time, the Merritt Parkway was being built by the State of Connecticut, and the state was offering much more money per acre than the BHC was giving to the residents of the Saugatuck River Valley. Environmentalists didn't have the strength back then that they do now, and despite protests from local towns and several groups of citizens, the BHC had the law on their side.

With the dam built and the waters about to rise, the BHC went about removing bodies from the local cemetery. They moved some houses to higher ground. The others were set on fire and destroyed. And in a few short months, the towns of Valley Forge and Hull ceased to exist as the waters rose.

The towns faded from memory and passed into legend. And as the ultra-rich sipped from the pure waters of the reservoir, they never considered what might still live beneath the waters.

While Gerald Roberts lay dying in a hospital bed only a few miles from where his family's small farm once stood, he handed his only grandson a note. On it, in finely written penmanship - indicative of the importance of the note - were the following numbers:

41°16'54.1"N 73°22'40.9"W

3271025

If you'd been on Rte. 53, just west of where the old church steeple of Valley Forge poked out of the water during droughts, you would have seen a man in SCUBA gear walking back to his truck with a smile on his face beneath the moonless night sky. After putting his tanks, a shovel, and an underwater flashlight into the bed of his truck, he placed the object he'd just spent the past two hours diving for onto the passenger's seat.

The box, made from the same solid iron ore that was once mined from this valley, had lasted almost 80 years beneath the ground and with the waters of the *Saugatuck Reservoir* on top of it with little wear and tear. If you'd been on Rte. 53 that night, you would have seen Gerald Roberts' only grandson thumb the combination to the lock on the box, and open it up. And inside, you would have seen something that was about to change this young man's life, and the life of most of the citizens of lower Fairfield Country, forever.

## The Lights Slowly Dim

*Week Twenty Three*

"I'm not coming back."

With those words, I watched as the stars unhinged themselves and crashed to the ground in shattered pieces of yellow porcelain. And in the nothingness she left behind, the cold black of the abyss, the thundering silence, I was presented with two distinct options. One, remain floating in the unknown. Two, jump into the void in a desperate attempt to search for the bottom.

Clenching my teeth and closing my eyes, I took the leap and found a world in reverse. Pain became happiness, the end was the beginning, and chaos unspiraled into a straight line.

## Death and Advertising

*Week Twenty Four*

I've made my living in advertising, more or less, for over 13 years. And in that time, I've determined one single truth: advertising needs to die. It's crumbling because of the agencies who overthink every last detail. It's ruined by the clients who care more about statistics and numbers than letting their brand stand for something. And it's obliterated by people like me: creatives who throw briefs into a meat grinder and pull out variations on the same complacent bullshit we've been spinning for years and try to call it *art*. Yes, my friends, advertising needs to die.

First, the *why*. We speak of the 50s and 60s as the heyday of the advertising "craft." Where brands had snappy lines, memorable commercials, and bold print campaigns. But once the jingles faded, and the art was replaced by the safety of recycling, advertising became just another line item in a budget. Brands no longer wanted to take risks. They no longer wanted to tread unexplored territories. What they wanted was what everyone else was doing. What they wanted was to get as many people to see their ads, but they didn't care if the message resonated with them. Advertising, at least our current form of advertising, needs to be destroyed.

Second, the *what*. The silent rule is this: the more exceptional, irreverent, or unique a piece of advertising is, the more likely it is to be killed by the higher-ups and clients. It's why all car commercials have their newest models peeling around turns on CA-1. It's why tech companies use highly reflective surfaces to show you the latest laptop. It's what everyone else is doing. You've seen it all in the chaos, and because of this wall of similar sights and sounds, your brand won't stick in the minds of consumers. So forget what the research says. Forget the key demographic you're trying to reach. Simply tell a unique story. Make something risky. Push the envelope, and the more you do, the more you and your consumers will be rewarded.

Third, the *who*. I work with genuine artists, people who astound me daily with their exceptional creations. But these "pieces" are dulled into something uninspired by a suit with an MBA. Someone who thinks they know what consumers want because of an extra few years of schooling. Masterpieces are turned into trite shit that might hit all the notes that the research seeks, but lack any form of interest. Let these artists astound you. Let them blow your mind. Enjoy the story that each piece has to tell without whittling it down to some unrecognizable lump of boredom. Clients pay agencies good money for the expertise, so get your money's worth.

Fourth, the *when*. Now. Seriously.

Five, the *how*. We can change the industry by killing the industry. Throw away your spreadsheets. Lose the statistics. Forget what you've been taught. Don't worry about how something "ladders up." Stop pretending your brand has a voice. Simply - just create. Make something beautiful. Make something daring. Make something that people will want to invest time in. Create art. And I promise the consumers will not only come, but they'll appreciate you more.

## No Such Luck

*Week Twenty Five*

Alleys are hard to find in Manhattan. Sure, Hollywood would have you believe they're filled with dumpsters, Spidermen, and homeless people, but usually they're just an alley in New Orleans, Toronto, or Vancouver made to look like the Big Apple. This thought sparked through Ben's mind briefly as he stumbled into just such an alley. A real alley. In real Manhattan. Without the benefit of a director to lead him through the next couple minutes.

Taxis were always hard to hail on 8th Avenue, but almost impossible when the bars were in full swing on a Saturday night. After fifteen minutes of trying, Ben lowered his arm, stumbled under the weight of too many beers, and began walking. His phone was dead, a result of him spending most of the night grumbling to himself about his overwhelming boredom and propped up in a booth playing Fruit Ninja as the phone's battery slowly drained. Uber was out, so was calling his friends who'd left hours ago. Instead, he pointed his body toward the New York Times building – the first beacon that would lead him toward his apartment on 18th.

And despite Ben's earnest attempt at using the Times building as a guide, he ended up here, in one of Manhattan's only alleys. A subway rumbled dozens of feet below him rattling the walls and causing the ladder of a rusty fire escape to sway and squeak. Ben picked up his pace, heading deeper into the alley in a backwards attempt to become less lost.

No. Such. Luck.

The alley dumped Ben out onto a dark street filled with shuttered warehouses and blinking street lamps. He turned around and decided to go back to where he came from. Another subway rumbled underfoot, this one seemed closer. When it passed, Ben felt like it pulled with it a vacuum of sound. Silence. No sirens in the distance, no honking, no steady roar from the Westside Highway. Ben blamed the beers.

In the silence, Ben realized one single thing: he was absolutely alone – save for that black shadow moving toward him down the alley. What the absolute fuck? Squinting, he could almost make out eyes, deep flaming eyes that punctured the blackness of the shadow. He turned around to see another shadow at the other end of the alley, only this one held a long shiny object that it dragged along behind it.

The second shadow took a step forward, the object behind it sounding like an aluminum baseball bat being pulled over asphalt, the clank echoed off the alley walls. Ben couldn't reach the ladder of the nearest fire escape, and there was no way in Hell he was running toward those... those... things. Instead, through a beer-battered brain, he determined his best course of action was to hide in between two dumpsters and wait it out. If things got bad, he figured he'd be able to reason his way out of it. Negotiate.

Clank. Clank. Clank. Clank.

The shadows were getting closer, converging on Ben. He closed his eyes, attempting to wake himself up from whatever messed up dream he was currently in.

No. Such. Luck.

The clanking stopped, and Ben opened his eyes. Standing before him were the two shadows – still impossibly black, as if the darkness were sucking the color out of the world. Their red eyes dialed in on Ben. A fiery jagged half circle appeared on the face – or rather, the spot where there should have been a face - of the one holding the metal object. Ben could only assume it was a smile. A sinister smile accompanied by a growling laughter.

He should have talked to that girl at the bar. He should have called his parents more often. He should have donated more to charity. He should have given money to that homeless guy on 23rd street.

And then he heard what was clearly a bicycle bell. The shadows moved back from Ben with a start, and focused their attention on the end of the alley. Another chime from the bell and the shadows erupted into a wail. Ben couldn't see who or what was ringing the bell, but whatever it was, it royally pissed these demons off.

Three. No four. Hell, maybe there were five who hit the pavement. Ben was in no position to keep count. He wasn't sure where they'd jumped down from, and with his position between the dumpsters he didn't have the best view. The sounds of swords being unsheathed came from everywhere. The wailing of the shadows only increased in volume. Crouching now, Ben held his ears while simultaneously bracing himself from whatever supernatural craziness was happening a few feet away.

Through his clenched eyelids, Ben could make out bright flashes of light, and felt intense heat far too close to his body. The wailing sounds turned to screams of terror. Whatever was attacking these shadows seemed to be winning. But then again, what if the other things were more evil than the shadows? Ben decided it was time to make a move. He didn't want to die in some forlorn alley next to a dumpster, and definitely not at the hands of whatever the fuck these demons were.

The action seemed to be taking place at one end of the alley giving Ben a chance to take the other end to safety. Peering around the corner, he saw fire, swords, dark, light, and most curious of all ... men. Whatever or whoever these things were, Ben didn't feel like finding out.

Focusing through an increasingly heavy headache, Ben pushed off the side of one of the dumpsters and made a run for it. With the freedom of a cold, dark, Manhattan side street in view, Ben felt for a second that he was going to make it.

No. Such. Luck.

His ankle was the first thing the shadow grabbed, tripping him. Ben fell to the ground with his arm and face breaking his fall. He turned to see what had grabbed him and was met with an ever-widening mouth of fire. Trying to kick, Ben couldn't escape the inhuman grasp of the demon ... and it was pulling him in. He reached into his pocket searching for something – anything – to throw at the thing. He came across his long-dead phone, did a quick cost benefit analysis, and threw it at the beast. Bouncing off the blackness, it only distracted the shadow for a brief second.

Bracing for his inevitable death, Ben closed his eyes and waited.

The slicing sound came first, followed by the roar of one hundred lions. Ben saw a silver sword pierce through the shadow, and the shadow let go of Ben's leg. Half crawling and half running Ben rushed out of the alley, knocking over a messenger bike, and took off without looking back.

Stopping a few blocks away, he saw a giant flash of bright white light followed by nothing. Silence. Darkness. For the smallest part of a second, he thought about going back to the alley to see what had happened, but an approaching taxi with its "For Hire" light on was heading toward him.

---

The light was brighter in the morning. It seemed to hit him directly in the eyes, perfectly traveling through the small slit in his blinds. A lovely way to start a hangover. Ben got up and grabbed some water. He needed some fresh air - something to help him figure out what (if anything) had happened last night. Lying to himself, he decided last night would be the last time he touched alcohol. Opening the door to his apartment, he almost tripped over a box sitting on his welcome mat. Wrapped in paper and twine, the only thing on it was a stamp that read "Wukong Couriers."

For a brief second, he thought about those signs on the subway that tell you to say something if you see something.

"Fuck it," and with that, Ben ripped open the box. Inside was his cellphone – fully charged – and ringing.

## First in Death

*Week Twenty Six*

John Haysmith is not what I expected. The tall and lean man enjoying a coffee in a diner booth in front of me and not far from his home in suburban Austin, is a contradiction. He's a far cry from the overweight hunched man sitting in his darkened basement, wiping Cheeto dust off his fingers and onto his pizza grease-stained shirt that I assumed he was. It's his hobby that instantly filled in the blanks of who I assumed he would be, but like most things on the internet, the truth is always different.

Haysmith belongs to a small and unaffiliated group of people from all over the world who partake in a daily contest. It's a dark and almost morbid activity, but the results are everlasting - at least until the internet or Wikipedia end.

Each day, Haysmith listens intently to the news. He prowls pop culture sites, and eagerly waits for a few distinct words to show up as an alert on his iPhone.

"Passed away"

"Has died"

"Will be remembered"

Once he sees these, he gets to work. "Is" becomes "was." "Dids" flood out of his computer. "Used tos" follow. And when he's done, and if he's quick enough, his name is immortalized in the canon of Wikipedia. John Haysmith is part of a small contingent of people who eagerly await the death of celebrities, athletes, authors, politicians, and notorious criminals, just so they can change the celebrity's' biographies in Wikipedia to the past tense. Once he's done, his name is plastered on the change log for that celebrity's page with a timestamp. And if he's been quick enough, his name will be next to a timestamp that's closest to that famous person's time of death.

"Michael Jackson is my white whale, so to speak," says Haysmith, shaking his head. "I updated Farrah Fawcett's page and basically shut down for the day assuming no one else of import would die on the same day. Then my phone blows up with news of Jackson's death about three hours later, but I was too far away from my computer to make any changes."

He may have missed out on updated Michael Jackson's page a few minutes after news of the King of Pop's passing hit the news outlets, but he is proud of those he can lay claim to.

"James Gandolfini, Carrie Fisher, Tom Wolfe, Charles Manson," Haysmith ticks of his fingers and a prideful smile appears on his face. "Sometimes we get false flags, you know, shitty reporting. I spent a good five minutes updating George H. W. Bush's page before it was confirmed that he was, in fact, not dead. [It] really bummed me out."

Haysmith's chief rival is a woman named Penelope Pemberton, a homemaker, who lives in the village of Leamington Spa in the UK. Just mentioning her name causes Haysmith to shake his head.

"She's a cheat. An absolute fucking cheat. She F.N.R.s and that's taking the art out of it."

I press him for the meaning of "F.N.R." and he explains how Pemberton copies the dead celebrity's page into Microsoft Word and does a "find and replace" to change all the necessary words to past tense. She then re-uploads the text into Wikipedia. It's quick, but not without errors. In the small community of self-styled "*Death Dockers,*" using tools outside of Wikipedia's editing software is considered a no-no.

"She got Bowie because of F.N.R. And I tell you what, his page was riddled with mistakes. Just because he no longer does something, doesn't mean his music doesn't continue to do something in the present tense."

*Editor's note: Penelope Pemberton refused to comment for this story.*

Haysmith's coffee finished and the check paid, he stands up and shakes my hand to leave. In his pants pocket, his phone vibrates quickly. Excitedly, he pulls it out expecting to see the horrible news of someone's death.

"Just the wife asking when I'm coming home." He puts the phone away and looks sullen, "It's too bad. I hear Kirk Douglas could go at any minute."

## Malin

*Week Twenty Seven*

I believe it's possible to pour all the waters in all the world's oceans into a juice glass.
I know the winds of a hurricane can be held back with a feather.
I trust that a flower hidden in a garden has petals of a color never before seen.

I accept all these things because you are proof of the impossible.

You slip hours between seconds.
You unlock all doors with your smile.
You take on infinity and count backwards.

You undid everything I understood about this world, and I'm better for it.

## Born This Way

### *Week Twenty Eight*

"You have to stick it in!"

"No way. No absolute way."

"Honey, it's the only way."

"Um... I didn't think it was going to be so large. Can't we call a doctor or something to make sure it's right?"

"We've gone over this, stick it in my butt! Make it quick!"

I should probably back up a bit. Like all the way back to Christmas of 2013. Lindsey and I were in Paris enjoying dinner at a small bistro just south of the *Place de la République* when the topic was first approached. To be honest, I'm not sure who brought it up. But it was super-poetic and full of drama - a world changing moment. And it went something like this:

"Do you want to have a kid?"

"Ok."

And that was it. We'd been married for a few years. We were getting older. We were finally financially stable. It just seemed like the right time. So below a deluge of French rain on a cold Christmas night, we decided to start a family with about as much fanfare as a parade featuring only one person playing a kazoo. We figured becoming parents would be easy and by the following Christmas we'd have a little one running around. But we were so very wrong.

---

The cup sat on my dresser for the better part of three months. Marked with a biohazard symbol and sealed in a sterile plastic bag, it was a constant reminder that not only would I have to do something rather gratuitous in a public place, but that my manhood was simultaneously being called into question.

We'd tried for a kid for over a year without any sort of success. Calendars were created. Plans were formed. But nothing seemed to work. So we made the decision to look for medical help. And before they could begin, they needed to run tests on both of us.

And this is how I found myself in a very small room a few weeks later, holding that very same cup, while a nurse informed me of all my different pornographic options. When I pictured conceiving a child, I expected it to be in a moonlit cabin standing over the tranquil waters of the Seychelles, not in a cramped room in Greenwich, Connecticut looking at the rolling hills of *Polly Peaks* while a group of nurses and my wife stood outside the door.

Left to my own devices, I was quickly nauseated by the realization that I wasn't the first to be alone in this room. As such, I didn't touch a thing. Videos and magazines were left in their drawers. I avoided chairs and walls. I even opened the door handle with the bottom of my shirt when it was finished.

Once all of that was over, my worries flooded in. Had I produced enough? ("produced" is the medical term, which adequately made me feel like a rubber chicken factory.) And most importantly, what if I was the problem here? What if my count was low? What if the one thing I'm supposed to be capable of I'm not actually capable of? So I silently handed off the cup to a nurse who looked like she'd heard every other joke made by every other nervous wannabe father, and met my wife in the waiting room.

"How'd it go?" She asked.

Now, this is a question that needs to be answered delicately, not unlike when a woman asks you if their outfit makes them look fat. Responding with a positive can come across gross and pervy. A negative would have been cause for concern. So I went with the first thing I could think of:

"It was voluminous."

Hair is voluminous. A body of work can be voluminous. But sperm in a cup should not be voluminous unless you're working with horses. Lindsey shook her head in a way that most wives who've come to understand the absurdity of their husbands often do, and we left the building.

---

Between the day of my - ahem - deposit, and the day they gave me my results, I took a long hard look at how I live my life. Should I keep my iPhone in my pocket where it can radioactively fry my testicles? Is there a way to blame this on my brother for kicking me in the balls as a child? Could my years spent wearing spandex and unisuits for rowing have inadvertently suffocated my sperm?

It turns out no. I was fine. My boys can swim. But the problem is, Lindsey was deemed fine, too. There's nothing medically wrong with either of us. And so we had to live with the very unscientific diagnosis of, "sometimes it just doesn't work."

So this, in turn, begs the question: was the universe trying to prevent us from having a child? Would our kid turn out to be the next Hitler? Were we brute forcing something that cosmically shouldn't be done - like drinking orange juice after brushing your teeth or listening to a Milli Vanilli album in the 21st Century?

But the good news was - and by "good news" I mean "let's deplete our life-savings because medical insurance won't foot the $30,000 bill" - we were ready to jump into the fun and exciting world of In Vitro Fertilization!

---

This brings us up-to-date. We'd been given instructions by the very patient nurse in our fertility doctor's office on how to administer the shots. They'd be daily, they'd be in Lindsey's butt muscles, and the gauge of the needle would look like a German railway gun.

Quick tip: don't go for the *Pulp Fiction* method of slamming a needle into anything, especially your wife's ass cheeks. You aren't trying to jump-start her heart after a heroin overdose.

So, on our first night of Progesterone shots, and once we determined that yes, this was the correct needle, I knelt down next to my wife's backside and stabbed her. Did I say, "Fuck fuck fuck!" while I did it? Absolutely. Did the act make my teeth hurt? Strangely, yes. Did Lindsey take it like a champion? 100%.

I will say that this process got insanely easier as the days and weeks went on. So much so that it became less of a tense horror film and more of a day-to-day occurrence like brushing your teeth or watering your rhubarb.

---

We were about six weeks in when we were told the pregnancy was going to fail. We'd put a lot of time, money, pain, and above all, hope, into this thing, and finding out that it wasn't going to work was incredibly defeating. We named the kid "Justice" just so we could say it was a "miscarriage of Justice" and hide our pain and frustration with humor.

But this made us confront a scary reality: what if this didn't work out? We only had three viable eggs, and the first one didn't take. What if the other two didn't either? Would we be comfortable being childless? Would Lindsey let me take the funds we would have used toward a college education and buy a Ferrari?

So... we took a few months off. We let Lindsey's butt recover. We let our hopes recover. And we tried again.

---

*"Are we out of the woods yet?" - T. Swift*

This song lyric kept echoing through my head each day since our second implantation. We'd made it past a few hurdles. The kid seemed to be doing fine. And Lindsey was beginning to accept the fact that she was about to spend the next nine months being pregnant.

Eventually, we realized we were out of the woods and headed toward a successful pregnancy, but then again, with a kid you're never actually "out of the woods." It turns out everything in the world can kill your child, and the only way to be truly out of the woods is to seal them up in a bubble.

---

Malin was born in the early morning hours of October 25, 2016. Healthy, happy, and perfect.

It took us almost 3 years to go from an idea to a fully-functional baby. Lindsey was a rockstar not just through all of the IVF, but the pregnancy and delivery as well. She's proof that women are stronger than men, and she gets 100% of the credit. Well, she gets 99% of the credit. Maybe 98.5% if we're being honest. I guess our fertility doctor gets some credit too. So she's at like 68.5%. Dr. Witt is about 30%. And I'm giving myself a hearty 1.5% for being an excellent butt stabber and/or public masturbator.

## Bending Toward the Horizon

*Week Twenty Nine*

My neck was stretched, head resting on the cushion of the backseat of my parent's station wagon. From there, I could see the glow of thousands of rectangles - each one encompassing a life. Driving up 3rd Avenue and over to the FDR, we'd make our way toward Connecticut as the dark of night fell over the city.

Each time we left, all I'd want to do is return. There was so much excitement, so much passion, so much more in New York City. And it was in those early 80's trips into the city that my life gained a singular purpose: I would one day live in this great town.

While my classmates drew pictures of dragons and army men, my pages were filled with pencil drawings of buildings; their maze of grey structures bending toward the horizon.

By the time I made it to New York after college, they were still hauling truckloads of lower Manhattan to Fresh Kills. It was a city looking to regain its footing. It needed direction. It needed to breathe. And because of that, we made an excellent pair.

It took me about a year before I considered it "home," and returning from trips in the country, I'd always be able to exhale once I rounded a corner and saw the skyscrapers of midtown rising in the distance. I've never felt so connected to anywhere I've lived. The pace, the movement, the rumble of New York just seemed to line up perfectly with what I needed out of a town.

It was the guy pushing an AM New York in my face as I walk to the subway. It was knowing my laundry man - whose name I'd never bothered to learn, having already pulled my name up on the computer and hauled my bag of neatly folded clothes onto the counter by the time I made it down the steps. It was Central Park, and Riverside. It was the sunset over the Hudson on Pier I. It was the futile attempts to catch a cab on 8th Avenue after a night at the bars. It was early morning bike rides down the Hudson, or brushing past picture snapping tourists in Columbus Circle. It was the museums and the galleries, the stores in the West Village and the odor of Chinatown. It was sitting in the center of the universe and being able to reach out and touch it.

I fell in love in this city - a town perfectly designed to generate love. And to think of the countless friends this city has given me requires a herculean effort. But really, it's that New York has given me so much, that in a small way I feel as if I'll always be a part of it and it of me.

I've never been able to accurately explain why I love New York to those who've never lived there. Most look at it like an act of self-flagellation. And really, while you can visit or work in New York, to truly *understand* New York, you must live here. You must breath in the air for years. You must *become* the city.

A decade after I first moved into Manhattan, a box truck filled with every piece of IKEA furniture I'd accumulated over the decade came to move me out. It was time to take the next step in my life and while my years in New York were legendary, I needed to, forgive the trite expression, find literal greener pastures.

With a silent nod to the city as the truck made its way over Triboro Bridge and toward New England, I told myself that this wasn't goodbye, this was just an expansion of who I needed to be.

And even now, out here among everything else, you can still find me bending toward the horizon.

# Light in Absence

## *Week Thirty*

Early Novembers in Vermont were a mixed bag. The ever-present low-hanging clouds gave off a chill that pierced bones. And the mixture of rain and snow that fell in equal measure layered the fields and roads with a brown mash of sludge that smelled of peaty organic decay.

I was playing with my G.I. Joes on the lowered tailgate of my father's rapidly-rusting Chevy C/K, and engineered a battle to take the hill of the truck's wheel well while my father was in the back of the town's hardware store getting his propane tanks refueled.

"Who's winning?" the cigarette smoke-dusted voice of Mr. Chambers fell like a slow-moving rockslide toward the back of the truck.

"The Joes. The Joes always win," I muttered back, still too engrossed in the battle and too impolite to turn around and greet Mr. Chambers.

My father placed the now-filled tanks into the bed of the truck, and issued a command that - based on the tone and force - I knew was not meant as a question. "Kevin, put your army men away, ok?"

I reluctantly grabbed my action figures, placed them in my jacket pocket, and finally made eye-contact with the worn and wet eyes of Mr. Chambers. Giving him a brief shoulder shrug, I huffed to the front of the truck, and hopped up into the passenger side to resume the war. I watched in the rearview mirror as he and my dad talked for a few minutes - wondering what it was that adults talk about.

As we drove back up the twisted and rutted road to my parents' home nestled on the side of a hill, I found the bravery to ask my dad why Mr. Chambers always looked so sad. He took a breath, and in the short moment between the inhale and his answer, I could see him arranging the words in a way that would make sense to my 8 year-old mind.

"Remember when I told you I was in the war?" he said.

"Yeah, Vietnam, right?" I responded, proud that I'd pronounced it correctly.

"Right. Well, I had it pretty easy. I sat behind a desk for most of the time and typed reports. I never saw any action."

"You didn't shoot anyone?"

"No buddy, I never shot anyone."

"Did Mr. Chambers shoot anyone?"

"Well, I'm not sure. But he was also in Vietnam and he didn't have it easy. A lot of his friends died, and that makes him really sad."

"But that was so long ago."

"Yes, but sadness like that doesn't just go away. You can be so deeply affected by it that it stays with you for the rest of their lives."

I looked out the window and watched as the rain and snow traced lines across the glass. My dad, clearly realizing that he, perhaps, had gone too deep on the explanation, quickly tried to explain himself.

"But you're lucky. You won't have to experience that sort of thing. We've learned from our mistake," and he punctuated the end of the conversation by turning on the radio and let the sounds of Eddie Van Halen and crew fill the humid air of the truck's cabin.

---

A few years ago, at the request of my father, I'd started helping out around the Meadowbrook Dairy farm. What began as mucking the cow barn, lead to setting up the Holsteins in the milking parlour. And at some point, I became Mr. Chambers' farm hand, for lack of a better term. And in all that time, outside of small instructions and greetings, we rarely spoke. So it caught me off guard when he called me into the small room off the parlor that performed as a makeshift office.

Instead of talking, he passed a document over to me and said, "that's it." I would come to understand later that the document, sent by the US government, was asking local farmers to sell their cows for above fair market value in an attempt to reduce competition among dairy farms. The cows would be slaughtered, and the farms would sit empty. But at that moment, while the metallic din of the conveyor belt set the tone as it ran behind the cows and carried their manure out of the parlor and into a heap beside the barn, all I saw was a numerical figure. A figure larger than I'd ever known, but one that didn't seem to affect Chambers.

"Farm hasn't been profitable for years. I can't really turn this down," he said, taking the paper back, folding it, and placing it in his worn wooden desk. "I expect they'll shut us down in a month or two."

Because we'd said so little, I was unsure how to proceed. If someone had presented me with that kind of money, my immature sense of worth would have taken it in a second. But I could sense a feeling of resignation, perhaps a touch of fatalism, from Chambers, and said the only thing I could muster, "I'm sorry."

I turned to go back to work, and saw the cows lined up in two rows down the center of the parlor, blissfully ignorant as to their fate.

---

The sap hoses arched between the maple tree trunks, drawing the sweet fluid toward the fill buckets scattered near the edge of the drive, and they looked like the skeletal remains of festive bunting that'd been ruined by too many Vermont winters. It was early morning, and the dull sunlight cast a deep purple over the fields as I drove the truck toward Meadowbrook.

The barns were empty - the cows removed by the truckload en route to an unspeakable death - and the stillness of the morning exaggerated each creak from a wooden slat on the barn, every footstep through the muddy drive left a *slock* and gurgle as I walked toward the entrance to the milking parlor.

Chambers had asked me to come and move some of the equipment he was selling off to a large farming conglomerate that was slowly buying up property in the area. I felt like I owed it to him - maybe I owed it to the farm - but we were in this together, and I needed to see it through to completion.

My father would tell me later that emptiness is crushing. "Sadness can be tolerated, but emptiness, true loss of everything, was detrimental and irreversible to the human spirit." And it was the first time that I understood Mr. Chambers' motivation.

Due to the danger of fires, the door to the silo was never left open. So when I saw it cracked, I knew something was wrong. In a way, my mind had already filled in the blanks as to what I was about to see. Brushing past the open door, I saw Chambers' feet dangling where they shouldn't be.

I turned around quietly, reverently, and phoned the police from the same wooden desk that Chambers had signed the sale of his Holsteins over to the government. Sitting in the silence while I waited for the sirens to grow closer, I found a small envelope with "Kevin" scrawled across the front in Chambers' handwriting, and hesitated for a moment - secretly praying I wasn't about to read his suicide note.

I opened it slowly, and wiped my eyes that'd already seen too much this early in the morning.

*Kevin,*
*Everyone will experience darkness in their life. But it's how bright you shine in the darkness that will make all the difference.*

*-Farmer William Chambers*

## Checked Out

*Week Thirty One*

Every once in a while they'd test you on a Diebold, but NCRs were mostly used for the physical part of the test. Lancelot Diageo had spent the last four months memorizing every key stroke, every arm movement, and even the pacing involved in correctly using one of the machines. He could practically perform the tasks in his sleep. But on his way to the testing center, he had a sudden freak-out. A notion that turned into a thought that became on obsession.

What if they changed it up? What if they used a Diebold? What if he failed?

20 minutes ago, failure didn't seem like a possibility. But as his Toyota Camry with autonomous driving capabilities and a crash test rating of 4.5 cruised toward the Center for Commercialism, Lancelot began to sweat. He was acquainted with Diebolds, sure, but he'd never practiced on one.

The line to get into the C.F.C. snaked down the brutalist concrete steps, and wrapped around the block and down the side street. Placed every six feet along the line were motion billboards advertising Xanax-infused hyper-distilled water, frontal-lobe surgeries for smart phone implantations, and vacations to the smokestacks of Bridgeport, Connecticut. The captive audience, inching slowly toward the testing center, would begin subconsciously memorizing the taglines and websites of each ad before they got inside.

Lancelot stood in line, and attempted to pull up information on the Diebolds while he waited. The C.F.C. had geofenced the entire block, removing all access to the internet, save for a few websites on consumer packaged goods, Amazon.com, and, strangely, a speech by the Minister of Sales about the evils of importation.

"Welcome to the C.F.C. My name is Eldridge Nike and I'll be your test proctor today. Let's begin." his name tag hung off his shirt, clinging with it's metallic claw to a small strip of 90% recycled material polymer fabric.

Lancelot ran through the test, answering question after question, and with each his smile grew larger. But no matter how well he did on this part of the test, he'd still have to face the physical test, and if he failed there, he'd fail the whole thing.

Eldridge chimed in with a simple "15 minutes to go," but Lancelot was already reviewing his answers, double checking them for accuracy. He hit the "submit" button on the screen, a brief advertisement played showcasing a new snack food derived from discarded trimmed cat claws, and finally a message popped up saying, "Lancelot Diageo, Your Test Has Been Submitted."

Once all the test takers had completed their exams, Eldridge walked the group down a long hallway and into a large room with large machines covered in purple cloths spread evenly throughout.

Eldridge stood on a small platform overlooking his test takers and spoke with a dictatorial cadence, "Ladies and gentlemen, I present to you the Diebold ST-580 Self-Checkout Machine." With that, small cables lifted the cloths off the machines and Lancelot's heart sunk.

Assistants stood at each machine with digital pads in their hands. The group was separated into lines of five at the head of each Diebold. Small grocery baskets were handed to each of the participants; each with a unique set of items inside.

Lancelot looked down at his, and saw two bottles of Dr. Lefty's Yellow Drink, a Passchendaele Memorial Mud Cookie Tin, and several boxes of Google AdWords Contact Lenses. He lifted it a few centimeters at a time in an attempt to determine its weight.

Two people stood in front of Lancelot. The first was a man of, at least, 90 whose hands shook with such a tremble that it seemed as if his remaining life were trying to escape through his fingers. Behind the old man, a young girl of 10 or 11 stood confidently.

"Begin!" shouted Eldridge over the masses.

The old man at the front of the line was handling things rather well. He scanned a box of Man's Best Friend Dog Flavored Dog Treats with ease. But his second item, a can of Bethlehem Steel Vienna Sausages wouldn't scan with his tremor-filled hands. The rest of us in line gasped when he reached for the "call for help" button - a death knell. The assistant came over and helped him finish. Once his items were bagged, two men dressed in black with wires falling from their ears came up to him with hands on their tasers.

"Sir, you'll have to come with us." they said in unison.

"Why? What have I done?" he pleaded through a weak voice.

"Sir, by the power invested in me by the Order of Sam Walton, you have failed to properly use a self-checkout machine. You are no longer able to contribute to society. You've been recalled." said one of the men with a flat tone.

As one of the men held the elderly gentleman, another went into his pocket, removed his wallet, and snapped his credit cards in half. Tears fell down the man's face. He looked up at the man holding him and pleaded.

"Please, I have grandchildren. Please don't do this."

Wordlessly, they dragged him away as his Stabe-L Cushioned Shoes with Reinforced Memory Foam soles squeaked along the pristine surface of the floor.

Next up, and with a slight loss in confidence, the young girl began unloading the products from her basket. She scanned her loyalty card with perfection, and placed a bag of Stevia Branded Apples on the scale of the Diebold as soon as she was asked. She was good.

But she missed the large box of Octopus-Derived Retinol Forehead Cream sitting at the end of the belt - no doubt a test by the examiner to see how she'd perform were a customer in front of her taking too long to bag their items. Alarms sounded and again two men dressed in black with identical ear pieces rushed toward her.

"Ma'am, you'll have to come with us," again, said in unison.

"But... but... but... that's not fair!" she sobbed. A small squirm in her attempt to release her arms from the men resulted in one grabbing his Shock Your Flock Taser, and running a few thousand volts of electricity through the young child. Twitching on the floor, and with drool escaping from her unconscious mouth, she was dragged away into a far off room to be recalled.

Lancelot stood at the Diebold. His hands shook. Sweat formed on his palms. His eyes were glassy. The examiner stood at the ready, prepared to mark any slight misuse of the machine into their digital screen.

Loyalty card scan. Done. Yellow drink scan. Done. The cookie tin scan required Lancelot to find the barcode on a strange section of the packaging, but he located it with ease and beamed it into the internal workings of the Diebold. Finally, the contact lenses scanned and were sent down the belt. Lancelot indicated that he'd like to pay with his credit card, and paused briefly - did the Diebold want you to insert the card or swipe the card? He couldn't remember.

The examiner marked something off on their pad.

"Shit," he thought.

Closing his eyes, he inserted his credit card into the chip reader. The examiner made another note. The receipt printed, he waited for it to finish, and ripped it off cleanly. He moved to the end, bagged his products and stepped away.

"Mr. Diageo?" one of the men dressed in black came up behind him. "Congratulations and welcome to consumerism."

---

Two days later, Lancelot Diageo found himself standing in a line at the self-checkout aisle at his local Shop More. He looked at the freshly burned barcode tattoo on his left wrist, and admired its design, its crispness, and its usefulness.

## Heathrow: An Explanation

### *Week Thirty Two*

*Currently, I'm in a hotel in the middle of London with my daughter who has just managed to delete the last story I wrote. I liked it. It was weird and off-beat. It talked about how you always know you're in the international terminal because the violent cacophony of smells attacking your nose will let you know that the many tourists who've sprayed too much perfume all over themselves are within convenient proximity to the Duty Free Shop.*

*But the story itself was one of obsessive curiosity. A man watches as women after women enter the woman's washroom, but none leave. None. And he starts to freak out about it. He even looks at what's happening architecturally - perhaps he missed something. But no, these women are disappearing into the women's toilets and no one seems to care. And the story ended with him opening the door - and committing the cardinal sin of being a man, that of never entering the women's washroom. And in truth, I didn't know how to end it. I hadn't figured it out. I almost think I would have just let it go blank. Let the reader write the ending in their heads.*

*But the fact is, it's lost. It was fun, it was entertaining, but it's gone forever. And so this is my first week without a story. At least a "real" one. I don't blame my kid, she didn't know what she was doing. But I do blame myself for typing this up while an excited two year old want to go out and explore the city.*

## Spark

### *Week Thirty Three*

*"How many fates turnaround in the overtime? Ballerinas have fins that you'll never find."*

-Tori Amos, *Spark*

You want to stick a giant middle finger to the sky and hurl insults to whichever chosen deity you're worshipping that week. How could they do this? How could they bring so much pain? Because this? This is unfair. This isn't right. This isn't how things are *supposed* to go.

I look for the symphony in the chaos. Something that ties it altogether and brings harmony to the unending nothingness. The religious will claim I'm looking for God. But what I think I'm really looking for is someone or something to blame. Something that can take the brunt force of hurt and leave me only slightly bruised.

And I know, deep in my heart, that nothing will answer. There will be no response. Because this pain is temporary. Heart-breaking, sure. But brief and fleeting. And when measured as a whole with the culmination of my incredibly privileged life, this is a speed bump. A quickly fading bruise on an otherwise perfect apple.

## Fortunate Sun

*Week Thirty Four*

0.6%. That's the amount of total land in the United States necessary to build solar farms to power the entire nation. 11,200,000 acres to generate 4,000,000 GWh of clean and renewable electricity. Solar Logistics knew this when they began buying up large tracts of cheap land in three locations across the almost always sunny American southwest. These would be the future sites of SunFire 1, SunFire 2, and SunFire 3, the largest and most-technologically advanced solar farms in the world.

The creation of SunFire would put an end to the coal and nuclear power industries, and it would, effectively, create a giant dent in the oil industry. That it made its way through congressional approval, passed lobbyists and politicians in the pocket of Big Oil, was no small feat and one that's attributed to it being a mostly private undertaking.

But Big Oil was not going down without a fight. They created bullshit papers about the lack of feasibility of the project. They created television commercials talking about the destruction of the American desert - ironically leaving out the part about the damages they themselves had done to the Gulf of Mexico and Prince William Sound. And when those didn't sway the public, they decided to take things a bit further.

Enter Dawson Ashgrove, former Special Ops, and now a "boots on the ground" guy for anyone with a big enough check book. He helped a few CEOs out of unwanted situations, both foreign and domestic, and had managed to sabotage the manufacturing abilities of an up-and-coming airplane builder that put them out of business within five months. He not only cleaned up messes, he created them too.

His arrival in Bisbee, Arizona with a few extra zeros in his savings account from ExxonMobile and blueprints of SunFire 2 in his Pelican Case meant that things were about to get very messy. The back of his Volvo XC40 had everything he needed for the job - high explosives, guns and ammunition, his trusty "for emergency only" box, and enough items and information to tie this whole thing back to a small group of Islamic radicals.

The plan was easy enough. SunFire 2 was still being built, so security would be diminished. Based on the surveillance he'd already performed, Ashgrove could take out the skeleton crew quickly and without much fanfare. From there, he'd plant explosives near the photovoltaic cells, destroying more than 70% of them. He'd take special care to rupture barrels containing sulfuric acid and sodium hydroxide, showing the public that solar energy was not without its dangerous chemicals. Finally, he'd leave behind a few documents and hard drives in his rented room that would point fingers at the known "persons of interest" who were thought to be in league with several oil-producing Middle Eastern nations. All of this would, hopefully, have the power to stop Solar Logistics in their track. By ExxonMobile's estimation, they wouldn't have enough cash to finish the project, and if they attempted to get public funding, none of this would pass through the Republican-controlled congress.

---

Dusk had painted the Mule Mountains a deep purple. He sat on a low hillock overlooking SunFire 2 with his M107 set up in front of him. There were six personnel in the complex, four inside, and one each outside at the gates. He'd be able to eliminate the two gate targets before either one of them heard the report from the gun. But this would send the four others into alarm. He anticipated at least two of the four to come out and look at what happened, making them easy targets. He'd then take out the remaining personnel once he got into the complex. Even if someone managed to call the Bisbee police, it'd be a half an hour before they could get out to SunFire. Ashgrove would already be gone, and the remote explosives would already be in place.

Two shots echoed off the photovoltaic cells, and two bodies lay motionless at the east and west gates. None of the SunFire crew were alerted, meaning Ashgrove would have to take care of them in person.

Had the other four personnel been watching the hills, the would have seen the XC40 driving down toward the west gate with a trail of dust rising up behind it. It smashed through the entry gate and stopped near the border cells. Ashgrove opened the trunk and placed the first unarmed explosive on the ground. He'd carefully designed these so that each were daisy-chained together with rope and priming wire so he could drive the truck and they would fall out the back in even intervals.

He serpentined around the rows of cells, his trunk getting lighter and lighter, before a bullet lodged itself in the truck's hood. Then another. Ashgrove immediately regretted not taking out the personnel first.

Instead of driving away from the gunfire, he drove toward it. The XC40 had kicked up enough dust that he was driving blind. And once he killed the headlights, it meant that his attackers couldn't find him either. Backing up and retracing his path, he heard the sound of gunshots in the distance, but none hit the truck. He took a different route through the solar farm, still laying out a string of explosives behind him. He then made a beeline toward the main building where the shots were coming from and winced as one landed in his shoulder. Two more tore through his front left tire and the truck fumbled to a stop.

Dust surrounded him again. Applying pressure to his shoulder, he ran around back and pulled the rest of the explosives out of the back. Three more gun shots snapped into the truck. He quickly set up the triggering device and armed the explosives. It was too late to remotely detonate. Small red lights illuminated in a twisted trail behind him and throughout the solar farm.

He could hear footsteps running up behind him. He pulled out his sidearm and fired wildly into the dust hoping to ward off anyone approaching. But when he felt the cold steel pressed into his temple, he knew it was over.

One press of the button sent a bright white flash that seared Ashgrove's eyes for an instant and then left nothing but an empty blackness that slowly turned off all sound and thought.

---

"Investigators have determined that it was rogue Islamic militants operating in cooperation with the Saudi Arabian government that caused the explosion at the SunFire 2 complex last month where six bodies were recovered from the blast. Solar Logistics, the owner of SunFire 2 has said that clean-up will take a few months and that the project is on hold pending further review. In other news, the makers of Dushenivan, a once-promising cancer treatment drug, have stopped development after five of its test subjects died as a result of using it in clinical trials."

# Hopyard

*Week Thirty Five*

The valley sunk lower and lower between the hills with each passing year. Weighed down by the gnarled oak trees with black leaves that seemed to absorb the wind, the river valley between Mount Tom and Leesville Hill was known by the indigenous people as "Machimoodus" or "the place of bad noises."

Thunderclaps, crashes, and deep rumbles would escape so frequently from this area that the Native Americans avoided it during their hunts. They blamed the terrors on Hobbamock, an evil deity who'd worshipped the dead and cursed the land, and the dark woods in the valley were left to grow and growl wildly without interference.

When the white settlers came to the region in what was then the Connecticut colony, they didn't hear or consider the warnings. They set up a mill next to the small stream that jumped through the valley and down its walls, and a young village with the anglicized name of Moodus began to grow in the musty air beneath the dark canopy.

But the noises never ceased. The newly arrived colonists blamed them on witchcraft, and insisted that the sinister dealings of Hobbamock were none other than the machinations of the Devil risen from Hell and looking for a few souls to take.

Deep in the woods, and echoing out of caves, the noises grew louder. Cattle were startled, families moved away, and crops were blighted. A meeting was called, and on May 16, 1791, a group of men from Moodus set off into the woods to confront the Devil and to banish him from their young country. Armed with lanterns and rifles, they set out into the thick forest and climbed the rolling hills as the sounds of rolling boulders grew louder.

---

The largest earthquake to ever hit Connecticut happened on the night of May 16, 1791. It toppled chimneys and church steeples. Windows cracked, and pictures fell from the walls. The water in the harbors of New Haven and Bridgeport crashed over the stones of the jetties and sent boats twisting on their moorings. The quake was felt in Boston and New York City, and was centered squarely in the woods outside of Moodus.

Each man who went into the woods that night never officially spoke of what they saw or what they did. Stories and speculation were passed down through the generations - all with puritanical and fearful leanings. Some claim the men found nothing. Others swear they saw the Devil dancing atop a waterfall as his tail burned potholes into the rocks below the falls, and they fought him before finally entombing him in a cave nearby. Others tell tales of the men bargaining with the Devil, and being bestowed with great wealth and prosperity. But whatever history you believe, the noises deep in the woods of Moodus went silent for generations.

Recently, two teenagers claim to have seen a figure dancing atop the falls at night with small fires lit on either side of the cascades. Small fissures have formed in the humid ground, and cracks have torn through nearby roads. And other residents have heard rumblings from deep within the earth, an unholy growl of rock brushing against rock as if a great furnace were relighting.

## The Storm and Cape Williams

*Week Thirty Six*

The bow of the ship cast its thin shadow down onto waters of the harbor in the midday sun. The fenders squeaked lowly as the slow rocking of the ship pressed them into dock, and the spring lines slacked with each roll. It had been years since the *Eventide* had been on the open water. Aside from the two or three storms that made their way up the Atlantic Coast each year and sent white caps across Cape Williams' harbor, the gentle up and down was the most movement the ship would experience on any given day.

The *Eventide* was ritualistically scrubbed cleaned each month on strict orders from its owner, P. Wellington Scott, better known as "Wells," the wealthiest man in Cape Williams who doubled as the town's local eccentric. He hadn't set foot on the boat since he'd purchased it a decade before, but as it was the longest and tallest boat in the harbor, and as it was a representation of who he was and the wealth he'd inherited, he felt the town deserved to have it looking well-polished.

The Scott family had helped settle the town generations before and quickly amassed their fortune through the creation of a textile mill spun for decades a few miles up on the Cape Williams River before moving their services overseas and eventually selling off the company to a multinational conglomerate. The remaining money filtered down to Wells through years of family in-fighting, divorce, and death leaving him as the only remaining heir. Rumors spread through town that he'd died in his mansion over-looking the town, but no one had the energy to go up to the house and find the corpse. But the checks kept coming and the so the *Eventide* was kept barnacle free.

---

*Ballyhoo* started as an idea. While on a bike ride, Aaron Peters had helped a blind man cross the street. The friends he was with mentioned how nice it was that he'd helped the man, but Aaron wanted more. He wanted the world to know just how nice of a person he was. And that notion sparked an idea that turned into an app that turned into a worldwide phenomenon which made Aaron Peters a lot of money.

*Ballyhoo* gave everyone with the app a chance to give points to friends, family members, and strangers based on the good deeds they'd done. Get a cat out of a tree and your friend might give you 5 *Ballyhoos* - the name for the in-app point system. Help a friend move, and they might reward you with 20 *Ballyhoos*. The higher your number, the more things that would become available to you. Insurance companies would lower your premiums. Soda companies would want you to give out free products to your friends. And people on dating apps might be convinced that you weren't a serial killer.

Aaron Peters (currently at 34,522 *Ballyhoos*) shunned Silicon Valley. He hated cities. He didn't like the idea of being landlocked in some midwestern farming state. And when his girlfriend (71,329 *Ballyhoos*) spoke about a cute little town away on the water named Cape Williams, his ears perked up.

Land was purchased. A mansion was built. And the citizens of Cape Williams spun the rumor mill up again.

---

The *Ballyhoo* was built in a shipyard in Holland and made its way across the Atlantic and into Cape Williams Harbor with much fanfare. Aaron hired a band, held a parade, and donated enough money to the local fire department to procure the use of their fireboat to "christen" the *Ballyhoo* as it made its way toward the dock.

As the crew jumped out to fasten the bow lines to their cleats, the diminishing wake of the ship sent the *Eventide* - moored to the other side of the dock - bobbing wildly. Several feet longer and a few inches taller, the *Ballyhoo* cast a long shadow over the *Eventide* in the late day sun. The townspeople were invited on board, and Aaron threw a loud and raucous party that lasted until the sun rose the next morning.

Up the hill, the thud of the bass and the tinny hits from the band's horn section were carried up on the wind and settled aggravatingly in the ears of P. Wellington Scott who sat in his chair on his balcony overlooking his town. He tossed his remaining scotch into the trees, slammed the balcony doors shut, and moved to the edge of his bed where he grumbled incoherently.

If you'd been on the Cape Williams docks a few night later, you would have seen him. Dressed in black, Wells walked silently along the wooden planks, with a flashlight in one hand and a tape measure in the other. He carefully attached one end to the space between two boards on the dock next to the bow of the *Ballyhoo* and ran it down to the stern.

"Damn it," he exclaimed looking at the tick marks on the tape measure. Aaron's ship was seven feet longer than the *Eventide*.

Three days later, the *Eventide* disappeared from the dock and a week after that, the *Eventide II* motored into the harbor. Longer, taller, and faster, Wells' new boat had the latest technology, a bigger engine, and enough bells and whistles to make the *Ballyhoo* seem insignificant in comparison.

In an interview with the *Cape Williams Courier*, the newly not-dead Wells explained that the *Eventide II* was a purchase a long time coming, and that he received an offer for his old boat that he simply couldn't pass up. When asked if he'd seen the *Ballyhoo* parked on the docks, Wells feigned ignorance and said he hadn't even noticed it.

Aaron Peters laughed at the article, and then went straight into his company's database to see what sort of *Ballyhoo* numbers this P. Wellington Scott character was pulling in.

His search came up empty. Wells was either using an alias or he - perish the thought - wasn't using the service at all.

---

The *Indian Scout Bobber* roared up the hill, the rumble from its dual exhaust shook the leaves of the trees, and from a mile away, Wells could hear it approaching. When Aaron got to the gate, he shut off the motorcycle, and removed his helmet. Locating the callbox, he pressed the button repeatedly, but received no answer from Wells huddled inside. Anticipating this, he pulled an envelope out of his jacket and taped it to the gate. Inside, a note invited Wells to spend some time aboard the *Ballyhoo* and mentioned that, as the two wealthiest people in Cape Williams, they should discuss how they can better the community.

A note was sent back to Aaron on Wells' letter head with a small typed-out message: No.

---

The *Ballyhoo* II's two personal water craft hung off the stern and added four feet to the total length of Aaron Peters new boat. Its flying bridge not only added height, but gave Aaron a perfect view down onto the *Eventide II*. He'd sold some of his stock in his company to make the purchase, but once he saw the boat at the dock, and the shadow it cast, he knew it was worth it.

---

The *Eventide III* had a helicopter. Wells sold off some of his property to afford the new yacht. The *Ballyhoo III* was a repurposed military ship used by the Argentine Navy and cost so much money that Aaron had to take out a second mortgage on his mansion. This back and forth continued for months until Wells had sold off most of his family's assets and Aaron Peters had liquidated most of his stocks. Wells hadn't slept in weeks; spending nights pouring over yacht catalogues and designs. Aaron Peters was so consumed with this ship-based cold war that he was asked by the company's board to vacate his position as CEO.

The two never met and never spoke. But the town of Cape Williams rejoiced at the increase in tourism (and taxes) at the escalation. People came from miles around to see the two largest private vessels on the East Coast. Wells paid to have a deep-water channel cut through the harbor to safely sail the *Eventide VIII* in while Aaron had land removed from the harbor-adjacent elementary school so he could park the *Ballyhoo VII* without its stern sticking out into the middle of the harbor.

---

An area of low pressure formed off the coast of Currituck Beach in North Carolina. This extratropical storm quickly gathered strength and by the time it made its way up the coast, it had become a bonafide nor'easter. Due to the geographic anomaly of Cape Williams and its precarious placement on the coast, it soon became apparent that the small village would bear the brunt of the storm. Weather stations urged residents to seek refuge while Cape Williams' harbor master instructed all vessels to relocate to less vulnerable harbors.

Every single seaworthy ship in Cape Williams was out of the harbor a day before the nor'easter arrived. All but two. The *Ballyhoo VII* and the *Eventide VIII* were so large that they couldn't move to a suitable harbor, and while the harbor master suggested that Wells and Aaron move their ships out to sea to ride out the storm, neither man knew how to sail.

---

Trees were torn from their roots. A storm surge ran through the stilts of the houses built along the beach. And an off-shore buoy recorded record wave heights. When the clouds cleared and the winds died down, the Mayor of Cape Williams drove through the limb-strewn streets and down to the harbor. Seeing the state of things, he immediately placed two telephone calls.

Wells and Aaron sat on the splintered dock looking out at the debris field floating in Cape Williams' harbor. Aaron reached down and pulled a broken wooden board out of the water. The letters "BALLYH" were clearly visible. He laughed, placed the board on the dock, shook Wells' hand, and silently walked back up the gangplank toward town. Wells smiled and stared out into the harbor. A board painted in the unmistakable red of the *Eventide VIII* floated by. He plucked it up, smiled, and rested it on the dock next to the remaining board of the *Ballyhoo VII.* A smile unfurled from his lips as he noticed, quite unmistakably, that the board from the *Eventide VIII* was at least half an inch longer than the board from the *Ballyhoo VII.*

## In the Forgotten Season, Chapter Four

*Week Thirty Seven*

The pandas looked happy. Cheerful, playing, and doing whatever anthropomorphic pandas do when they're committing one of their children to a psychiatric hospital. Absent were the chihuahuas in straitjackets, the lemurs lining up to take their pills, and the kangaroos slamming their furry heads against the walls of the padded rooms.

The book, titled "Welcome to Elmcrest" or "The Insane Asylum and You" or "So, You Decided to Kill Yourself" was an attempt by the authors to describe to new patients (and their siblings) what to expect during the first few days at Elmcrest Hospital through peaceful illustrations of pandas interacting with teachers, doctors, and fellow mentally ill and possibly suicidal animals. My parents pushed it across the table to me and said, "This is where Eric is going to stay for a while."

I remember thumbing through the book awkwardly, not so much reading it as coming to terms with being an only child for the first time in my life. On the one hand, my brother was horribly ill, but on the other hand, I would no longer be "Eric's Brother." I could reinvent myself. I'd head into fifth grade as a new man, one who'd escaped the long shadow of his better looking and more charismatic brother.

I secretly hoped it would take a few months for him to get straightened out. I needed enough time to establish myself amongst my peers as the new alpha male. Machiavellian ideas began to form in my head.

"Adam! Adam!" my mom was looking worn, "are you listening to me? We're going up there on Sunday and you need to come, too."

"To this hospital?" I said, absently pointing to a photo of a smiling panda picking flowers on a hillside.

"Yes. It'll help get him settled in."

---

Elmcrest sat on a steep bluff overlooking the Connecticut River in Portland in the shadow of a high bridge that crossed the river a few hundred yards away. When choosing a location to build a hospital full of suicidal children, they couldn't have picked a worse spot. One would expect to find already-tied nooses hanging from rafters or an air-tight warehouse with constantly running automobiles on the property.

To gain entrance into the hospital, you first passed through a gate and checked into the main office. Then, you were walked down to a separate building where a series of locks, doors, and chaperones would get you progressively closer to the main room. Decorated in bold colors, and designed with a mid-80s aesthetic, the goal of this modern area was to provide light, warmth, and security to seriously ill children, while erasing the notions of the turn-of-the-century asylums that plagued the country.

The main room was built next to a courtyard and had a series of bedrooms built off of it. The more a patient "progressed" through their treatment, the better and more private their accommodations became. Eric started off in a room with six to eight other kids and had a small corner next to his bed to "personalize" with safe objects from home - that were neither sharp or heavy.

The hospital was about an hour's drive north from our house in Fairfield, and my parents created a schedule of visitation throughout the week that allowed them to be present in his life on an almost-daily basis, and brought me into the fold twice a week on Thursdays and Sundays. The rest of the time, I was looked after by friends of my parents.

On my first trip to Elmcrest, one thing became very clear to me: I needed to help Eric escape. Completely forgetting *why* he was in such a facility along with the clear fact that I was way too weak, small, and stupid to pull of such a feat. But the idea of my twin brother being held behind locked doors didn't sit well with my 10 year-old mind. And so I went about planning our escape attempt.

Step 1: We'd need to hurdle the wall in the courtyard. To do that, we'd need to hop up on something, like a table, chair, or other patient.

Step 2: We'd make a run for the river and head downstream away from the hospital until we reached the swing bridge in Haddam some *dozen miles* to the south. And yes, I get the issue now. Why didn't we just take the bridge *next* to the hospital? Well, you see, that's what the hospital staff would anticipate. And my little pre-pubescent mind had considered that. But what it didn't consider - or, one of the many things it didn't consider - was that bringing my heavily medicated and sick brother miles down a river was a *horrible idea.*

Step 3: We go on the lam.

Yes, I understand. This is a shitty plan. I mean, hell, I drew maps and escape routes in crayon. And let's assume we somehow make it out of the heavily-guarded hospital campus. Let's pretend I was capable of carrying my brother toward our destiny. What then? In my head, we'd somehow make it to Disney World and spend the rest of our lives living in a fantasy dream world where nothing bad ever happens. But considering we had about $1.25 between us, and I hated sleeping outdoors, the plan was quickly doomed to fail.

But that didn't stop me from pulling Eric aside and telling him, "You know, I can get you out of here if you want. I've got a *plan*."

And his reaction was appropriate for a 10 year-old going through the most difficult part of his young life, "Yeah, no. I'm good here."

And that's when the strange notion finally occurred to me. Eric needed this place. He wanted to get healthy. This was the right place for him. Sure, he shared a room with a kid of tried to burn down his parent's house too many times, and another friend of his tried to slice his own throat open with a broken ketchup bottle, but right now, Eric didn't need me. He didn't need to sleep at home. He didn't need to escape. He needed to get better.

As we drove home, a tear fell down my face as I stuttered out a question that had been devastating the back of my mind for weeks, "Eric is going to get better, right?"

My mother, in her stoic and forceful optimism, turned around and said, "Absolutely," without another word.

And I believed her. This was a strange time for our family, and 25% of us were not driving home in that car that night. But I understood at that moment that sometimes you need to break something apart to put it back together better than it was before.

## Poke

### *Week Thirty Eight*

Before you go assuming anything, know that I've spoken with experts. My college roommate attended med school for a few semesters. I've consulted charts and watched YouTube videos. This should work.

The tools have been disinfected. I have bandages. I have painkillers. My phone is dialed to 9-1-1, I only need to hit "send" if something goes awry. But I assure you, nothing will go awry.

It's very simple, really.

I'm about to drive a nail into my skull.

This isn't some carnival magician's ruse. I'm not slamming a nail into my nasal cavity. No, I'm using a hammer and nail to create a *Burr Hole* into my forehead ... and I'm putting it on *YouTube*.

*9:32pm*: This is the start. I've used a Sharpie to mark a small "X" where I want to hammer. Based on what I see in the mirror in front of me, I'm guessing it's about an inch above my brow and dead-center. This is a good spot. It should cleanly miss the supratrochlear artery.

*9:34pm:* I'm trying to build up the nerves. The 1,442 live viewers on my YouTube channel are helping.

*9:35pm*: I've got the nail held firmly between my left thumb and index finger. I guess it's just a matter of taking a swing.

*9:36pm:* Lots of blood. More than I was anticipating. But I can't get the nail to stick in. I think the angle is wrong.

*9:42pm:* I've sat here for the past few minutes with a bandage pressed into my head trying to stem the bleeding. But it gave me time to think. I'm going about this wrong. I need an external force to get the nail stuck in my head.

*9:48pm:* It's set up. I've used chewing gum to stick the nail on my forehead. To get it into the bone, my plan is to take a running jump head-first into the wall of my kitchen. Let's see how this goes.

*9:49pm:* Missed.

*9:50pm:* Misssed.

*9:51pm:* Nail fell out,

*9:52pm:* got it

*9:54pm:* It's probbaly a few millimeters in. Im gonna usue the hammer to finnish the job

*9:55pm:* Lotof blood

*9:59pm:* paain

*10:01pm:* I cant foowwe but its oo kk

*10:03pm:* oto a kf o ai

## Thunderclap

*Week Thirty Nine*

I pulled him aside and told him, in no uncertain terms, to knock it off. We were at a party, we were drinking, and he was being way too "handsy" with girls who clearly indicated they were not interested. That's when he put his arm around my shoulder and said, "Dude, it's ok. I'll tell you more when I'm not so drunk, but I'm untouchable," explaining that no matter what happened tonight, he was above the law. He came from a wealthy family, had a privileged upbringing, attended prestigious schools, and felt as if he were shielded from consequence.

But me and other party attendees saw him make attempts. We saw where he was trying to go. And luckily, we made sure to let him know that not only did we not approve, we'd stop him far before it ever came to him sexually assaulting someone.

But I've witnessed this behavior too often from too many people, and while it's not just privileged white men who commit sexual assault, it seems like there's a plethora of them who think they can get away with it unscathed.

Our President has made comments that would suggest he's sexually assaulted women (see: "I grab them by the pussy"), and has several sexual assault claims against him, while his current Supreme Court nominee has three against him. So we're definitely in a climate where rich powerful white men have gained even more power despite some serious charges. This isn't a new phenomenon. Look at Michael Skakel and Alex Kelly - two wealthy white men who used their privilege to escape prosecution only for it to come crashing down on them years later.

And yes, Skakel and Kelly eventually saw justice prevail and a new crop of men are feeling the wrath of their actions (Cosby, Weinstein, et. al.), but why is it that these men feel like they're above the law? And why has it taken so long for the repercussions of their actions to finally come to light?

The truth is, we as a society are to blame. We've let it happen. Growing up, these men are taught to be masters of the universe. To be unstoppable forces as they reach for glory and riches. They are told they deserve everything and that consequences are only for those who can't afford the right lawyers.

So, how do we stop this systemic righteous selfishness? It's quite simple: we don't let them get away with it. We hold them accountable for their actions in the moment - despite whatever sort of inebriation they're experiencing. We pull them aside at parties and let them know. And we sure as shit don't elect them to office.

Dr. Ford did a remarkable job during her hearing yesterday. She was poised, calm, and heart-breaking talking about such a horrible act. And she proved to not just women, but all people, that talking about sexual assault, telling people, and putting yourself out there as a figurehead gives so much power back to the victims. I'm sure it'll inspire hundreds more to come forward and not let their attackers get away with it.

Sexual assault attempts aren't going away. But it's up to us as friends, as co-workers, and human beings to stop someone, to pull them back, to take a second and explain how horrible and selfish their actions are. And despite the pain, we need to talk about these things. We need to be informed. Because if we don't, these people will happily ruin someone's entire life for a few moments of sexual gratification.

## The Convert

### *Week Forty*

Five miles north of Barstow, there is nothing. An emptiness that stretches past the horizon and into oblivion. A few crumbling mountains that were once held under and pounded by the risen ocean. And a chemical taste that rides on the air currents and sticks to the back of your tongue existing somewhere between salt and sulphur.

This is where Jessica came to lead her people. Surrounded by a vacuum, she could fill that void with her spirituality. There was nothing to distract her followers from her teachings, and her proximity to I-15 meant she could entice some sinners traveling between Los Angeles and Las Vegas. Five miles north of Barstow, Jessica found her heart, her nerve center, and her purpose.

The stories of how she got here differ. Some say her car broke down, others say she just appeared. All agree it was a divine providence. No matter how she got here, she wasn't going anywhere.

She introduced herself to local townspeople. She networked. Her friendliness spread. And she accumulated enough donated money to build several small buildings on scrubland donated - unknowingly - by the United States government.

And this is when the miracles happened.

In the confusion, they were documented by several of her followers who settled their discrepancies with their individual stories before publishing them outright. According to her disciples, she was, apparently, able to raise livestock from the dead. Her birth coincided with a solar eclipse. She was able to read minds. Some claim to have seen them in person. Others heard about them from someone else. All agreed that Jessica was put on this planet to change the world.

She sent letters to leaders, urging for peace. She condoned violence and oppression. And with a healthy mix of eastern and western religions, she firmly planted herself in a small section of desert as a savior.

News reports went out. Rumors spread. People flocked. She cloistered those closest to her and wrote scripture. And at the end of one of those meetings, it became apparent that, to continue the spread of her message, she'd have to become a martyr.

Preparations were made. Theatrics were put in place. It would appear that she was assassinated by members of the Catholic Church - two birds with one stone - she insisted. Her followers believed it would help crumble the remaining stalwarts of the Catholic church, and help establish her new religion as the de rigueur.

As her motorcade passed through Boston, a single bullet entered her neck, and exited out through the opposite ear. She fell quickly. But the miracles continued. Followers claimed they saw her walking through the streets. They'd see her in a crowd. The felt her presence. And with each of these sightings, her religion grew.

---

Jessica's boyfriend left her on the side of the road en route to Las Vegas. She was in some shit town, filled with dust, and a lot of heat. She should have never gotten involved with Brent. She moved to LA for him. Hell, she dropped out of veterinary school for him. Now, she was penniless, with a dead phone, wandering a sweltering town and asking for help.

She made a beeline for the local restaurant, hoping she could pray upon the simpletons of the town to lend her some cash. She needed just enough to get back to LA. Maybe a couple hundred bucks.

Five feet in front of Edna's Cafe: Barstow's Finest Dining Establishment, Jessica turned on the charm. When she walked in, the room lit up. She did a lot of things poorly, but being enthusiastic and outwardly friendly were not one of them. She avoided talking about the circumstances that got her here, nor where she was explicitly headed - figuring these "small town folks" would hate "big city types." But by the time Edna's shutdown for the day, Jessica has $500 in her pocket and a room to stay in that night.

She decided to stay in Barstow for a few more days to see how things went. After all, she had no place to go - not really anyway - and all the time in the world.

Weeks passed and the charity continued. A neighbor was ridding himself of his extra trailer, which Jessica readily accepted and parked on land north of the town.

She was enjoying her second cup of coffee that morning at Edna's when she'd heard a rancher talking about an ill calf. Having spent a few years at veterinary school and with a general idea as to inner workings of a cow, she offered assistance.

A quick review of the calf's diet (lacking in selenium), and she established that it was suffering from nutritional muscular dystrophy. A suggestion on new grasses and a few injections later and the calf was up and walking around. The farmer hailed Jessica as a hero. A misinterpretation by the nosy townspeople led her to be hailed as a savior.

Instead of balking at such a notion, Jessica embraced it.

People were lining up. And like her flock, her message grew. She spent a few nights writing down what she wanted people to do. Simple things that she hoped would make the world a little bit better. She's seen the shitty parts of this planet and hoped to spare others from those. She read the Quran, the Torah, the Bible, and a severely abridged version of the Tipitaka - highlighting the passages and notions she liked best. She then regurgitated them into her weekly sermons.

5 miles north of Barstow, Jessica's religion grew.

Buildings were built on the government land - and realizing that removing these people and their illegal construction would result in a full-scale war, the U.S. let it go.

They were walking through the newly-built sanctuary when Jessica told her closest advisor that they needed to prepare for her death - her martyrdom. They arranged everything, including the place, the perpetrator, and the other religion that would take the hit for her assassination. In order to build something new, you need to destroy something old. In Jessica's case, it would be the Catholic church.

As her caravan made its way down Arlington Street to the west of the Boston Public Garden, a shot entered her car and killed her almost instantly. For theatrics, they raced the car to Tufts Medical Center where she was declared D.O.A., but the body was dead well before they got to the hospital.

In fact, the body was dead before the shot rang out. The body was dead days before.

She was handpicked by Jessica months before the "assassination." She was dying anyway, and felt like sacrificing herself to spread Jessica's message was more important than the extra few months of life. And silently and painlessly, she'd passed away in a church days before the trip to Boston with Jessica by her side.

The assassination made worldwide headlines. The "perpetrator," a Catholic "radical" who - unbeknownst to the world - had recently converted to Jessica's religion and was now happily on trial for murder.

And from the shadows, Jessica watched it all. She saw her image spread around the world. She heard words she'd spoken months before, poured over, bastardized, and repeatedly endlessly. The donations continued to pour in, and, in exile, a large chunk made its way to her - a girl with nowhere to go and all the time in the world.

## Entanglement

### *Week Forty One*

*The oil ran out. Religion faded. And yet, man still found reasons to go to war.*
*-Danielle Zysmarek, The Book of Auger*

There were still "boots on the ground" but more in an attempt to keep civil peace or to stop under-funded military campaigns in third world countries. The armed forces were no longer, for all intents and purposes, needed. Global warfare became fully automated, and from there it evolved into battles played out between computers.

The simple version worked like this: one country did something to another country. Maybe they insulted their leader. Perhaps they hacked a social site. Whatever the cause, one country would declare war on another country and put up collateral in escrow. Land. Cash. People. Then, the two governments would "go to war" with each other, by means of calculating a complex series of equations using all the computing power they had in their arsenal. The quickest country to reach the answer was the winner and the losing country's collateral was turned over. Of course, this became more complicated when alliances were formed and other countries could combine their computing power to process even faster results.

Wars were over in the blink of an eye. Populations could cough and find themselves members of a new country. While this proved to be a dramatic reduction in wartime violence, it also meant that all computing power was now owned wholly by the government. You could be mid streaming-video when your country declared war on someone and suddenly, your computer, your tablet, or whatever you were watching on became "bricked" while the computation ran. That document you were working? Gone. That website you were surfing? Temporarily shut down. Computer privacy? A thing of the past.

As with any type of battle, this new computational warfare gave rise to a rebellion. Those who created CPUs that existed off the central grid. Home-built processors that ran the gamut from playing games to attempting to topple governments. Security forces nicknamed "Leechers" by those in the rebellion sought to find these underground computer engineers, take their processors and add them to the national collective while imprisoning those who built them. Often, their prisons were nothing more than work camps where they were forced to build more processors via slave labor.

Enter Davian Shaw. Shaw went underground after watching his partner Calisto and his life's work get absorbed by the Leechers. Quantum mechanics physicists by trade, Shaw and Calisto were hard at work developing a *non*-theoretical quantum computer. World governments saw their work, and when Calisto declined to give them the blueprints for their device, the Leechers found him and took it and him.

But Calisto hid a failsafe inside their device, one they returned it to a theoretical quantum computer rather than a working one. And by the time the Leechers realized they didn't have a working device, Calisto was dead and Shaw was on the run and off the map.

---

The European Front went to war with the Joint Argentinian State. Based on a territorial dispute over solar-harvesting sites in the Falklands, the war saw both sides "put up" 500,000 people and the entirety of the Falkland Islands. It took the JAS .0021µs to generate the computational answer as opposed to the EF's .0087µs.

500,000 members of the EF suddenly found themselves part of the JAS along with the Falklands (and their solar harvesters).

Davian Shaw watched the war play out in real time from his ghosted CPU somewhere on the island of Santorini. He'd arrived here more than six months earlier, after months of crisscrossing the globe to shake the Leechers. Santorini proved to be an ideal place to hide. It had ample sun which meant ample harvesters which meant ample energy. After the Greek government collapse in the 20s, Santorini existed as a small nation-state and existed outside the purview of the European Front. And, perhaps most importantly, Shaw's house was set into the cliff hundreds of feet above the water-logged caldera, and the only entrance to his residence was from above. This meant he could make a quick escape should one of the motion sensors go off above him, and quickly belay down to a fully fueled boat hidden among the rocks below.

The JAS victory in the Falklands was really just a stunt by the EF to reveal how much computing power the JAS possessed. They figured losing a few islands, some solar power, and half a million people was worth it. It exposed what kind of computing power they needed to have in order to take over the JAS entirely. And JAS proudly showed their hand.

Rumor had it that there was someone hiding out in southern Europe who just so happened to possess the fix for the failsafe blocking the quantum computer. The EF deployed their best Leechers throughout the region hoping to find the needle in the haystack. Once they found him, unlocked the computer, and went to war, the entirety of what was once South America would be theirs. It would be just a hop, skip, and a jump from there to grab the rest of the world.

And just before midnight on October 25th, Davian Shaw's motion sensor went off.

## The Snows of Baghdad

*Week Forty Two*

He grew up in the shadow of the stacks. Giant twisted industrial tumors that ripped into the green hills of the Pennsylvania countryside and expanded outwards into the waters of the Lehigh River. Bethlehem Steel was always there. A lumbering presence that chugged away in the background and fueled the town's economy. But when steel manufacturing went overseas, and along with it jobs, the town of Bethlehem lost its critical I-beam.

Tony grew up assuming he'd work at the steel mill just as his father and grandfather had before him. But when they closed the factory in 1995, he discovered that he'd have to find another employment option after high school. He spent four years working on cars, staying just-this-side of trouble, and dragging his feet aimlessly into the future. And when the World Trade Center fell, he found an out. He signed up for the Army National Guard, not out of any sort of patriotic duty, or a call to arms, but because it gave him something different to do.

He'd never been east of New York City let alone across the ocean. But Tony found himself sitting on a plane heading toward Iraq with the single drive to exist outside the shadow of Bethlehem - and if he happened to kill a Taliban or two, well that would just be an added bonus.

---

He was referred to as "the Asset" and Tony was instructed to never call him by his first name. He'd been stationed at Camp Cropper for more than three months, and in that time, he'd only caught a few glimpses of the man. Tony received word that he'd be rotating to direct guard duty - meaning he'd be stationed just outside the Asset's cell.

Tony was introduced to the man who looked older and more fatigued than the news footage made him appear. He spoke with an accent, but Tony was surprised by the Asset's knowledge of English.

"Hello Tony. I'm Saddam," the first words the dictator ever said to the boy from a town in eastern Pennsylvania. The rest of the day, and into the rest of the week, Tony and Saddam simply stared at each other - feeling each other out.

At night, Saddam would light up a cigar and listen to the radio, and during the day he'd read from the pile of books he kept next to his bed. It was during one of Saddam's nightly cigars that he finally broke the silence.

"Tony, would you like a cigar?" he asked, gesturing an unlit cigar toward the soldier? Caught off guard, Tony stuttered out, "Uh, no. No thank you, sir."

"Too bad. These are Cohibas! Best in the world!"

"I'm sure. But no thank you." Saddam placed the cigar back in its box and walked over to the bars, letting a small cloud of cigar smoke twist in the wind as it flowed behind him.

Leaning on the bars, Saddam asked, "Where are you from Tony?"

"Pennsylvania, sir."

"Does it snow in Pennsylvania, Tony?"

"Sometimes. We'll usually get a few snowstorms each year."

"Excellent. I've only seen snow a few times. It's a beautiful thing. It makes the world quiet. Nothing else can do that and be so beautiful."

"I suppose so, sir."

"I'm not one of your superiors. You don't have to call me 'sir' Tony."

"Right, sorry sir," Tony's time in the Army couldn't shake him of formalities.

"Do you have a girl back in Pennsylvania?"

"Uh. I had one. We broke up a few months after I deployed."

"What was her name?"

"Chris. Christine."

Saddam stubbed out his cigar and gave one last exhale, "Sorry about Christine, Tony. Any girl who won't stick around with you while you're in the Army probably isn't worth it anyway."

Sergeant Hicks walked in, and Tony stood at attention.

"Everything alright here Private?" Hicks looked directly at Saddam, "This guy's not giving you too much trouble?"

"No sir," Tony responded, "All is well, sir."

"All is well, huh? Well alright," and Hicks walked away. Saddam winked at Tony and went back to reading his books.

---

Saddam returned from one of his many "trips" during his incarceration. These were almost always his many times to stand trial for his various crimes. Each "trip" would occur at random times, and take random routes under heavy guard to throw off would-be assassins. When he got back to his cell, his worn and frayed suit hung off his thinning body. He sunk on his bed and rubbed his eyes.

"Tony, is your father proud of you?"

"I don't know. He left when I was young."

"So he doesn't know you're in the military."

"No, at least not that I know of."

"I bet he would be proud. You're a good child."

Images of Uday and Quesay, Saddam's sons and their grisly deaths flashed before Tony's eyes. Tony had wanted to tell Saddam he was sorry about his sons. Sorry about his grandson. But he didn't know how the old man would react, and he lacked the confidence to say anything.

---

Saddam was talking to Private Coppola, and they were both laughing, when Tony walked in.

"...He was mean. But he was funny," Saddam trailed off as Tony entered.

"Tony, you've got to hear his stories about Castro. They're legendary," Coppola was hanging on one of the prison bars.

"Mean man" Saddam repeated.

"Alright, I've got to take off. You're in good hands with Tony," Private Coppola gave Tony a friendly slap on the back and walked away.

Tony sat down in the chair outside Saddam's cell, and stared at him.

"Tony? Everything alright?"

Tony had heard more and more about the crimes being leveled against Saddam. The news was flooded with them lately. Unspeakable atrocities that Tony struggled to attach to the man he knew. The man he was supposed to protect with his life should anyone overthrow the compound.

"I've heard some things, man. Things that they're saying you did."

"There's a lot of stories. Some of them true. A lot of them not true."

"But how could you live with yourself?"

"Being a leader is hard, Tony. You can't make everyone happy."

"There's making people happy and then there's killing people."

"Yes, I believe it was more in the hope that things would be better for more people in Iraq if a few people died. Politics is never clean. Someone has to get hurt."

"But those people..."

"Look where I am, Tony," Saddam cut him off, "I spent the last year moving undercover. My family is gone or dead. I'm in a cell, and in a few short months, they're going to execute me. I've done some awful things. I have regrets. And I suffer because of those regrets."

"They say you're a monster."

"I AM a monster. But to lead these people. To lead this nation, you need to be a monster. You need to be forceful."

"By killing your own people?"

"My own people? They weren't my people. This country is not filled with my people. Before the First World War, Iraq was full of different tribes. But it was the British and the French who got together and decided where and who to put into this country. We didn't choose. One day, Iraq was just here. And people who'd spent centuries fighting each other now had to be part of the same nation? It didn't work out nicely like that."

"OK, then why did you kill MY people?"

"Tony. I didn't kill your people. In fact, I kept those who wanted to kill your people from committing such terrible acts."

Tony felt himself getting heated. He opened up his bag and took out the book he'd been reading - a thriller sent by someone back home. It was all he could do to end a conversation he didn't feel like losing.

In front of him and behind bars, he heard Saddam shuffle back to his chair and exhale loudly.

---

Rotations came and went, and it was in mid-December that Tony got word of his. The past few weeks, things had been tense between he and Saddam. They'd rarely spoken. He sat in his chair and took out his book. Before he'd even read a single word, he heard, "Tony? Tony?"

Tony looked up and saw Saddam standing at the bars looking at him.

"Tony, someone said you're leaving. You're heading home."

"I am."

"I will miss you, my friend. You are a good person, a good son, and you've been very kind to me."

Tony was taken aback. He wanted to apologize for the way he acted. The actions this man had done made him seethe with anger, but he knew only of this worn and feeble old man. He found it so hard to equate the two.

"I've enjoyed our time together, Saddam. I hope we'll see each other when I return."

"Saddam smiled a knowing smile, "Yes, I'd like that."

---

During the ride back from Newark International Airport, Tony stared out into the leafless trees that lined I-78. These leaves had fallen, and Tony let out a muffled laugh when he thought about how they'd just get replaced in the spring. As if the fall never happened.

When the truck pulled off the highway and made its way into the steel grey cold of the December Pennsylvania countryside, he wondered how he'd ever fit in here again. Everything was the same here, but he'd seen the world. He'd done more than he ever imagined he would. How would JJ at his old mechanic shop react when he told him he guarded Saddam Hussein? Hell, how he'd become friends with one of the most powerful men in the world? JJ would probably float a racist comment, shrug his shoulders, and wonder where the party was happening that night.

Tony woke up in the morning of December 30th and walked into the living room and found his mother watching the news.

"Tony. Come here! You're going to want to see this," she said, gesturing him to sit on the couch next to her.

He squinted toward the television and caught view of grainy footage of a man putting a rope around Saddam Hussein's neck. He picked up the remote and turned off the TV despite his mom's objections.

Tony walked out into the cold December morning, looked up in the sky, and felt wet flakes of snow land on his face. He watched as they swirled in the wind and blended into the white oblivion.

## The Bishop of Channelwood

*Week Forty Three*

He placed screws along the rubber edge that stuck out of the toe of his Doc Marten boots. They were short enough not to hit the floor, but long and sharp enough to damage the shin of anyone unlucky enough to be on the receiving end of one of his kicks. He was tall and lanky, with arms that hung lower than they should have. His face was marked with acne scabs, and his teeth never seemed to fit correctly inside his mouth. He'd assigned himself a nickname - Bishop - one that, he thought, added a level of mysteriousness to him, and generated a level of fear and or reverence as he walked the halls of his high school.

I'd never said one word to him.

I knew he was troubled. I knew he was angry - afflicted with the same "the world doesn't understand me" attitude many other white boys in my upper middle class suburb found themselves to suffer through. And I knew to stay out of his way.

My friend Blaine asked if I wanted to join her in her art class for the last period of the day. As it was quickly approaching the end of the school year, most teachers let their students fuck-off, especially if you were in art class. Faced with the option of staring out the window for 45 minutes in the boredom prison of study hall or hanging out with Blaine while she drew pictures, the choice was easy.

When she sat me down, I was right across the table from Bishop.

"Nice necklace," he said to me, pointing to the beaded orange, green, and black necklace I'd made the previous summer, "can I have it?"

"What? No," I responded, more confused than anything.

"I want it," he insisted, a spray of spit launched out of his mouth as he punctuated the "t" in "it."

I'm sure I laughed this off. I probably made a joke. If I'd known anything in my 15 years of life, it was that I wasn't a fighter. I could throw words around, but when it came to throwing a punch, it just wasn't my style. I'd been punched and kicked throughout middle school. I was tripped, thrown into lockers, and called names. But since I'd been in high school, I assumed that was all behind me. I'd spent freshman year free from physical assault.

Blaine was deep into her project to realize and the teacher was too distracted or too apathetic to care that things were getting heated between Bishop and me.

"I want that fucking necklace," he repeated, and the intensity in his eyes revealed that this wasn't a joke. I felt my hackles raise. My heart beat faster. I quickly went through a list of things to say to him to, to do to him, but alas I was too much of a coward and too much of a pacifist to sufficiently respond to him.

And that's when he took his boot and raked the sharpened screws down my exposed shin. Instantly, lines of blood gushed from the wounds and my socks filled with blood. I felt tears hurling toward the edges of my eyes. And I wanted to cry. I wanted to punch him. I wanted to yell, and claw his eyes out. I wanted to be anywhere but in that art room, sitting across from a teenage psychopath with parental issues, and I didn't want Blaine to see me cry.

And so, I reached behind my neck, unscrewed the clasp, and gave him the necklace. Bishop laughed. I told Blaine I needed to take off, that'd I'd forgotten something in my locker. Instead, I limped home (which was conveniently located a few hundred yards from school), and shouted "FUCK!" at the top of my lungs in the woods separating the school from my neighborhood. I tended to my wounds, threw out my socks, and vowed revenge.

My mind raced. I thought of all the ways I could harm Bishop. The things I could do to embarrass him. How, if I could be so lucky, I'd kill him. Kids like Bishop, they were a waste. They didn't deserve life. I'd get a gun and I'd put a bullet in Bishop's head.

---

My parents did an amazing thing during the Christmas of 1993. They bought me *SimCity 2000* and *Myst* to play on our *Macintosh IIci*. One game let me build my own world while the other let me explore other worlds - and both let me escape from my small section of suburbia. I'd spend so many hours alone in front of the computer and lost in these worlds that, when asked to describe me, my brother would say, "I don't know. He just sits in front of the computer all day."

The "nerds" in my school didn't play *Myst*. They were into comic books, and *Dungeons & Dragons*. They played *Doom*. And when I casually mentioned that I played *Myst* - they scoffed. What I didn't tell them was that I had a *Myst* poster in my bedroom. I owned the *Myst* novels. I drew maps of my own "ages," and spent far too much time actively reading up about the upcoming release of *Myst*'s sequel: *Riven*. It seemed, even for the geeks in my high school, I didn't possess the coolness to join them. And so, I explored and discussed the intricacies of *Myst* alone.

*Myst* was an escape for me. It gave me these strange islands to walk around, and look at the 3D rendered butterflies. It let me wonder what sort of things were beyond the horizon of suburbia, and it did it in a completely non-violent way.

On the day of my incident with Bishop, I went home and fumed. I daydreamed about inflicting violence. I happily imagined Bishop in various states of distress. And then, I turned on *Myst*. I walked to one of my favorite sections of *Myst* island, stood on the shore, and stared out into the (non-moving) ocean listening to the digital sounds of water lap against the beach.

And I calmed down. I escaped. Deep within those polygonal shapes and simulated natural noises, I found peace. I didn't need to shoot zombie Nazis. I didn't drive cars over helpless pedestrians. I just walked in what - some might argue - is a glorified slideshow, and took a deep breath.

---

Bored at work one day, I fell down the rabbit hole of looking up past acquaintances and co-workers on Facebook. And, purely out of morbid curiosity, I searched for Bishop. I half expected him to be dead, or so addicted to drugs that he couldn't muster the mental fortitude to build a profile. What I found not only surprised me, but left me delighted.

Bishop looked happy. There were pictures of him smiling with his wife, of being incredibly enthusiastic about the birth of his child, and details about him running his own art gallery. The angry kid I knew in high school had transformed into a respectable man who seemed to have his head on straight. And while Facebook tends to be an incongruous and optimistic peek into the lives of semi-strangers, what I saw on the surface of Bishop's adult life seemed genuine and loving.

I thought about the day he took my necklace and damaged my shins, and I can still remember the pain and anger I felt, and how I wanted to cause him retributive harm more than anything. But those scares are gone. And the more horrible thought is: what if I'd gone through with hurting him? What if I didn't take the time to take a deep breath and sit in a simulated island on my family's computer screen? While I had zero access to guns or knives, what if I'd tried to destroy this punk kid? I would have prevented the world from having another loving father. Another inspired artist. Another devoted husband. And that is truly horrifying.

## The Book Club

### *Week Forty Four*

Their cars were too big. Giant European behemoths made almost exclusively for soccer players and rich American housewives. With chairs wrapped in the skins of almost extinct African mammals, and a climate controlled system that simulated the delicate atmosphere inside the Vatican archives. They had names like Diane and Carol, and they were acutely aware of their position high atop the socio-economic food chain.

What started as a club to review books recommended by television talk show hosts while imbibing in rosé, quickly turned into something more sinister. And it started when Susan arrived at the book club with a dented bumper and what appeared to be blood on the grill of her Range Rover.

She said it was a squirrel. Then a coyote. Then she settled on it being a deer. She'd hit it while she was texting her daughter Kamryn about setting up Kamryn's appointment to get lip injections. Kamryn, being 13, felt like her mother was pressuring her into getting them. But just as Susan typed out, "Kam, I don't want the other mothers to see my daughter with thin lips and think I'm a bad parent" she'd hit ... it. Something big. Something no longer moving.

Instead of going out to check on it. Instead of calling the police, Susan drove on and parked at Brenda's and mentally prepared to talk - in depth - about the complex love triangle at work in *Tender Lusts*.

They were deep diving on chapter 27 when Tabitha's need for sexual gratification from her boss comes to a head when Susan broke down.

"I can't. I just can't. You guys, I think I killed something with my car."

And with that, all seven women found themselves staring at the front of Susan's Range Rover and discussing what she possibly hit. It was when Brenda pulled out an unmistakable human tooth from the carbon fiber hexagonal pattern of the grill that Susan smiled.

---

They agreed not to tell anyone. Keep it a secret. Let the poor fool who decided to jog in the dark on a twisty Connecticut back road suffer. They cleaned off the car, and off the six women went into the night.

Susan hadn't felt so alive in years. She gripped the steering wheel of her land tank and floored it around and over the rolling hills that littered Fairfield County. She kept a watchful eye out for anything and anyone crossing her path. She wanted nothing more than to feel the bone-pulverizing impact once again.

Brenda couldn't fall asleep. She tried to peg down what it was that kept her awake, what strange emotion it was. Because it wasn't fear. It wasn't anger or sadness. And around 2 o'clock in the morning, after much contemplation, Brenda decided she was jealous.

On Diane's drive home, she began breaking for a squirrel that ran out ahead of her Lexus, but replaying Susan's smile over in her head, wrath funneled through her muscles as she gunned the SUV and found a satisfying bump and crunch as two tons of Japanese steel popped the life out of the poor woodland creature.

Carol, who was admittedly the most shook up over Susan's revelation, rolled down the window and tossed her copy of *Tender Lusts* behind a stonewall that separated the road from a horse farm. She was too proud to associate with the book club anymore.

Sharon's husband hadn't come home in a week. He was either in Hong Kong, or Singapore, or Kuala Lumpur. She couldn't remember and she didn't care. With her kids asleep, Sharon listened to the silence of her home. And that's when the idea struck her. She went to the garage and stared at the front of her X5 with a glass of scotch in her hand. She slowly and drunkenly searched her garage, found some rope, a pitch fork, and a box of nails. Once she was done, the front of her BMW looked - while not exactly like something out of *Mad Max* - like it could do some serious damage to anyone who came into contact with it.

Kimberly stood in front of her *SubZero* as it cast its welcoming light over her collection of *All-Clad* pans, glimmered off the polished marble back splash she'd imported from Italy, and twisted and turned as it refracted off the neatly organized bottles of various artisanal oils she'd purchased in New York. She was chewing on a hangnail trying to stifle her want of food. Nothing in the fridge seemed to please her appetite. She wanted something else. Something more. Something raw. And with that, she found herself driving her G-Wagen back and forth in the approximate location that Susan had her accident. Once she spotted the blood on the road that trailed off into the woods, she instinctively wiped a line of drool from her lips, stopped the car, and walked off into the moonlight.

Finally, Paula drove her Porsche Cayenne back towards her gated community. On the way, she began texting Brent - the guy she'd met during a girls' night out - and with whom she'd been having an affair for the past two months. He'd sent her a dick pic and when she attempted to send him back a topless selfie, she slammed into a deer turning it into a cloud of red dust and sending her SUV spinning. Regaining control, she pulled the car over, finished sending the selfie to Brent, and took a look at the front of her car. It was drivable, but destroyed.

---

Kimberly was hosting the following week's book club. When the women showed up - including a reluctant Carol - each had something different about them. Something primal and excited. They distractedly tried to discuss the ending to *Tender Lusts*, but the topic kept returning to Susan's accident the week before.

And that's when the curiosity spilled over, and they split into two groups while piling into Paula's new Jaguar F-Pace and Sharon's BMW X5. The sun was quickly setting, and they determined the best place to find joggers would be on the road that ran along the beach.

Sharon spotted him first, a man in his mid-30s wearing earbuds and running at a good clip away from them.

"He'd never know what hit him," thought Sharon.

She aimed the pitchfork tied to her bumper at the jogger, and with her friends cheering her on, she gunned the accelerator. The pitchfork hit him just above his tailbone, ran through his abdomen, and exploded through his running shirt. He had only a split second to know what happened before being pulled under by the truck's massive wheels that crushed what remained of his body.

Both cars stopped. Excitedly, the women ran to the man's remains and tossed what they could of him into the ocean. Kimberly placed what appeared to be part of his shoulder into a Ziploc bag she'd brought along for just the occasion. They threw the damaged pitchfork into Sharon's trunk, cleaned off the car as best they could, and went on their way.

Paula's target was near the nature preserve. She tagged him quickly, and in her haste, she accidentally spun him off her hood. He landed in the grass on the side of the road, and was still alive.

In the back of the car, Brenda said, "Uh, Paula, he's still moving."

"Let's end this!" shouted Paula, throwing the car into reverse and landing the car's left back wheel directly on the man's back. Carol opened a bottle of champagne and poured it into the plastic travel glasses she'd taken from Kimberly's pantry.

---

The following week, Carol hit two people - teenagers - walking by the side of the road. Diane took out a coyote and a bicyclist near the Inn.

Susan bought books of stickers for the group, small emblems they could put on their fenders. Not unlike a fighter pilot's victory markings or a football lineman's quarterback sacks, each represented a kill. At the end of the summer, Sharon was leading with 8 followed closely by Diane's 7. Book discussions gave way to topics like body disposal, car bumper reinforcement, and which SUVs provided the most torque.

Despite the increase in front end damage to SUVs across town, the local police chalked the uptick in vehicular manslaughter to texting while driving. Plus, hefty donations by several prominent families in the town to the department's Police Athletic League forced them to lay blame on kids from the poorer towns in the region.

Late in September, the book club was out in force. October 1st was the end of the "season" and they'd decided to crown a champion - the woman with the most kills - on that date. And it was on a backroad near the country club that everything came to a head.

Paula opened her car door as she bore down on her target. The door slammed into the man, shattering the door's window, and wrapping him like a reverse "C" around the satin grey body work. Paula peeled him off, and placed him on the ground. Walking back to the car, Paula was working out how best to angle her car in order to finish him off. From the backseat, she heard Carol say, "Oh fuck!"

Carol had only met him once or twice, usually during their children's horse shows at the Hunt Club, but through the ruined flesh on the man's face, she recognized him without question. The man coughing up blood and spitting out teeth was Sharon's husband.

Sharon was with Brenda and Kimberly on the other side of town, but when Susan called her to tell her the news, she made Brenda beeline it toward the country club.

"Sharon, I'm so sorry. I didn't know. I didn't..."

"You killed my fucking HUSBAND, Paula! MY FUCKING HUSBAND."

"Yes, I know. But I… I… I didn't know he-"

Sharon grabbed Paula's cable knit sweater and threw her to the ground. She was on top of her slamming her in the face repeatedly with the horribly expensive diamond ring the dead man next to her had bought her 15 years before. Blood poured out of Paula's nose when Susan finally pulled Sharon off of her.

The next day, Paula - with swollen eyes and a broken nose - went out and put a new kill sticker on her fender.

---

No one expected Sharon to show up at book club the following week. Her husband's funeral was that morning, and no one had heard from her since the incident. It was October 1st and the women had decided to call it a draw and award champion status to both Sharon and Paula, who, despite killing someone's husband, still deserved the credit.

But out in the driveway, they heard the loud roar of a V8 engine. Behind the wheel of an electric yellow Hummer, Sharon was revving the engine as fire flashed through her eyes. As Paula, Susan, and Carol approached, Sharon threw the truck into gear and slammed all 5,000lbs of American overcompensation into the ladies.

Stepping down from the truck, Sharon calmly held the mangled wrists of each woman checking for a lack of pulse. With a smug satisfaction, she went back into the Hummer, grabbed something out of her purse, and placed 3 more kill stickers on her fender.

## The Currents

*Week Forty Five*

JinJo, the Man of Many Beans, brushed his dusty beard and heard the small kernels hit the rocky earth below his feet. Each time he inhaled, he swore he could taste the burnt remnants of giraffes - forever carried on the trade winds across the ocean. It had been many years since the Light, since the fire, and since the disease. It'd taken almost everything he had - including his sight - and left him with the only thing he now knew: loneliness.

JinJo had travelled three days out from Stone Town, and following the cordgrass shores of the estuary, he felt - no - he *knew* he was close. The years of searching, of following the wind, of chasing down rumors and stories, had led him to this point deep in the shadow of the *Dairugger*. The ions in the air twisted in charged fractals, and danced in the rhythm of the universe.

The girl with the metal teeth was here.

---

Charlotte's lip was bleeding. Years of repeated slicing and puncturing had rendered the inside of her cheeks heavy with an almost impenetrable shield of scarred skin. But every once in a while, she managed to catch the leading edge of one of her braces on her lip and send a scarlet line down her chin. She assumed it happened while she and BART were running after a cat near the wrecks. And really, Charlotte was running; BART was more like a hyper-caffeinated pogo stick having lost her leg, but not her drive, during the weeks after the Light. Charlotte held a tattered and dirt-stained sleeve to her mouth in an effort to stem the bleeding.

"Where the hell did it go?" Charlotte asked, squinting in the sun in search of a small black creature climbing over one of the dozen or so rusted husks of oil tankers that had crashed and were lately decaying on the shore.

"Beats the hell outta me," BART responded in her unmistakable southwestern Greenlandish accent, "Saw something up on the wheelhouse, but it might have been the wind."

"Well, then we go up."

The higher they climbed, the clearer they could hear them. A chorus of out-of-tune whines that sounded like a Satanic bellows stoking a chaotic fire: cats. Hundreds of cats. They exchanged knowing glances, and once setting foot on the tilted floor of the bridge and smelling the Sancerre-tinged scent of cat urine, they knew they'd found him.

---

Dr. Havestock couldn't play sports. He never played the piano. And despite his father's collegiate legacy, he couldn't grip an oar handle. Born with impossibly small hands, Havestock spent his childhood and teens pulling on his fingers in the hope that it would encourage growth. The brochures advertising boathouses slowly disappeared from his parent's kitchen table, his father hung up his scull in the rafters of their garage, and the wooden oars he'd planned on giving to his son made their way into a bonfire during one of the elder Havestock's drunken pity parties.

It wasn't until his non-scholarship provided days in college that he discovered the one thing his deformity had blessed him with: the ability to reach easily inside people's mouths. Bobby Ballhousen was in the dining hall four fifths of the way through a chicken leg when the bone slipped and lodged itself three fifths of the way down Bobby's throat. Two fifths of the way down the table, Havestock, stood up, walked slowly over to the choking Ballhousen, and used his minuscule hands to pull a slimy grey chicken bone from Bobby Ballhousen's throat.

A witness to this spectacle, Dr. Garber Van Garber, the head of the university's Department of Orthodontics, put down his one fifth finished shepherd's pie, and ran over to Havestock. Placing his arm around the student, Dr. Van Garber excitedly spoke about the wonders of orthodontic sciences, and specifically how one who was blessed with such impressive hands would succeed so tremendously.

Many years of schooling later, and Dr. Havestock opened his own clinic helping to correct every overbite, malocclusion, and crowding in the tri-county area. After the Light, and with most of his tools destroyed, he found himself without purpose once again.

Drifting through the coastal plains, he settled in a boneyard of half-eaten tankers and container ships, where he could feast on the marsh grasses, hide from the marauders high in the bridge of the *Dairugger*, and use his small hands to milk the cats that took refuge inside the derelict.

---

Charlotte pressed the back of her head deeper and deeper into the dental chair. Any millimeter of distance she could put between her and Dr. Holt, her orthodontist, would be beneficial. She was only 12, but knew enough to be, in her words, "skeeved out" by the man. He always spent longer with the girls, and his breath reeked of coffee and herbal penis enlargement pills. Despite his occupation, his mouth looked like the inside of a granite quarry.

"Yep, you've got one hell of an anterior crossbite," said Dr. Holt pushing back from the chair. His cubist teeth aligned in the closest thing they could to a smile as the doctor imagined not only the thousands of dollars he was about to fleece from this girl's parents, but the many sessions he'd get to spend with her while watching her teeth shift around her skull. "You're going to need braces."

The rite of passage for any pre-teen white suburban child, braces not only ensured you physical pain as they resculpted your skull, but mental pain as everyone you came into contact with would see the row of medieval torture device-like food magnets jutting out from your face.

Charlotte's life was over. At least for the next 2-3 years as Dr. Holt's diagnosis indicated.

On a sunny Tuesday morning, Charlotte sat in the very same dental engine as Dr. Holt and his two "I only dance to put myself through orthodontist assistant school" assistants attached the braces to her teeth. Charlotte instantly had a headache, and she spent the next five hours re-learning how to close her mouth.

As the sessions and years went on, Dr. Holt's diagnosis increased in length. 2-3 years turned to 4-5. And finally, as Charlotte sat in the waiting room of

Dr. Holt's practice on the day she was to get her braces off, the FBI raided the office and took Dr. Holt away in handcuffs.

Charlotte would be spending the foreseeable future with her dental work until she could find another orthodontist. She'd heard of a doctor north of her town, one who did amazing work, but the Light happened before she could track him down.

Now, 15 years on from the Light and 20 long years with braces, Charlotte had found the man who could finally remove them.

---

Dr. Havestock sat in the darkness listening to the ocean waves crash through a breach in the hull hundreds of feet below him. He saw the women climb up the *Dairugger's* tower, heard them enter the bridge, and grew nervous as his collection of cats turned silent. His fingers were too small to hold a gun, and the various tools he had on board were too small to do much damage in a fight.

The one missing a leg spoke first, "Dr. Havestock? We've spent years looking for you. We need your help."

He shifted uneasily in his perch.

The second one with the strawberry blonde hair spoke, "Dr. Havestock? Please. It's incredibly important."

When the woman spoke, Dr. Havestock saw something he hadn't seen in years. Something that brought him back to a time before the Light. Something that made him gasp audibly.

The woman with the strawberry blonde hair had braces.

---

BART sat on the side of the road. The partially burnt wooden oar she'd used as a leg rested broken and splintered next to her in the sand. She removed a can of *Ogdens' Nut Gone Flake Tobacco* from her backpack and shoved a wad of it into her bottom lip. She was still three weeks out from Stone Town, and with one leg and not a whole lot else, she'd decided this was a good spot to die.

Maybe someone would come along and give her a proper burial. Say a few words about her unknown life. Talk about things that never happened to her. Maybe an animal would feast on her corpse, return her to the earth - a real *Circle of Life* type of moment.

She dove blissfully into her recurring dream where she was riding her bicycle through the roads of her hometown of Kangerlussuaq with her radio mounted to the handlebars. She'd listen to the stations out of Kangaamiut, Eqalugarssuit, and Qaqortoq as she rode, with two working legs, along the shores of the fjord. And then - water. In her face. Enough to wake BART from better times.

"I seriously hope you're a pirate. Or, at the very least, someone who cosplays as a pirate. You're missing an opportunity here if you aren't," said the mass of colored lines standing over BART.

"What the fu- who the hell? Who are you?" Bart wiped her eyes, squinted into the sun and began to make out the woman standing before her.

"I'm Charlotte," said the woman, reaching a hand down to BART, "And you're coming with me to Stone Town."

"No. What? No! Leave me here to die. I'm shit company. I've got one leg. And I've determined that this shall be my final resting place."

"How about this?" Charlotte took a seat next to BART, "You come with me to Stone Town. I promise not to ask too many questions. And when we're done, I'll bring you back to this exact spot so you can kick the bucket."

"Really? You're going to use a term like 'kick the bucket' with an amputee?"

"Sarcasm. I like it. Come on, let's get a move on before nightfall."

BART launched a comet of brown tobacco spit into the sand, exhaled, and stood up. "Name's BART."

Charlotte looked at her skeptically.

"Yes, BART. And before you do what I know you're about to do, let me remind you that you said 'no questions.'"

"Technically, I said I wouldn't ask A LOT of questions. But fine. Nice to meet you BART. Let's go find an orthodontist in Stone Town - no questions asked."

---

JinJo felt his way along the rusted metal pipes. He carefully sidestepped open expanses that dropped into oblivion. Occasionally, he'd startle a cat which would hiss and run off into the maze of twisted metal that remained of the *Dairugger*. Despite all the metal, he could still feel her presence. A pulse of white flashed quicker in the dead ends of his optic nerves as he got closer and closer.

He pulled a kidney, a black-eyed, and a pinto out of his pocket. He'd need the protein for the climb up to the bridge.

---

Dr. Havestock, moved slowly out of the darkness. He sidestepped a few waiting cats, past shelves of vacuum tubes, diodes, a stationary bike, and a row of batteries. He raised his small hands above his head, all the while never taking his eyes of the strawberry blonde girl's mouth.

"You... you have braces," he stuttered incredulously.

"Yeah. No shit," she quipped.

"It's just that... it's been so long since I've seen them."

"Yeah, well they've been an absolute pleasure to have for the past 20 years. And as much as I love them, I feel like it's time we parted ways. That's why we're here."

BART hobbled forward, "I've spent the last five months listening to Charlotte complain about these things. So if you can't remove them, I'll just grab some of your pliers and give it a shot myself."

Dr. Havestock felt a spark at the back of his neck. He hadn't felt useful in years. "Of course. Uh... let me just get my tools."

His small hands tentatively gripped a worn leather satchel. He placed it with a rattle onto the wheelhouse's chart table and began removing rusted items from within. Charlotte stared at the mess in skeptical horror.

"When was the last time you had a tetanus shot?" he asked.

"You know, I was just going to get one the other day, but I was too busy sipping giardia-laced water out of the runoff pond from a decommissioned nuclear power plant - what with it being the end of the world and all."

"Right. I'll go slow."

---

JinJo, slightly out of breath and fumbling forward along the tilted floor of the wheelhouse, tried to shout. It had been years since he had spoken, and all that came out was a tiny whisper. It was enough to stir the collection of cats patiently waiting to be milked by the orthodontist with tiny hands, and their cries alerted BART, Charlotte, and Dr. Havestock - who'd just started poking around the scarred insides of Charlotte's mouth.

BART jumped over to the blind man, and helped guide him to a dilapidated captain's chair. Dr. Havestock brought him water. Charlotte, with her mouth held open by numerous rusted torture devices, could only gum out vowels in protest.

Barely audible and with a sigh of relief, JinJo said, "Thank you. I've come a long way for this. For her," and he pointed an old bony finger toward the strawberry blonde woman with a face full of metal.

Charlotte attempted to say, "Oh fuck no!" but all that came out was, "Oh uck oh!"

"I mean no harm," JinJo continued, "You have something I need. Rather, your braces do."

He spun a wild tale about how high-quality stainless steel was an almost extinct commodity these days, and how he'd heard tales about Charlotte and her mouth full of the precious resource. He needed it, he claimed, to use in radio transmissions. These broadcasts, he said, would cross the wastes, the shores, and oceans, and help bring unity back to the remaining people of planet Earth.

Charlotte mumbled something unintelligible.

"OK, so let's do it," BART said, pointing toward Charlotte, "Let's pull it out and give it a shot."

"Well, it might work better if we left the metal in her mouth," JinJo said, "and used her saliva to aid the conduit and the cavernous space of her mouth would make an excellent amplifier."

"oh ay. oh! Asouey ot. et e uck out o ere ol a," Charlotte protested.

Dr. Havestock looked around the bridge of the *Dairugger*, and quickly did an inventory. Quickly, and silently, he went to work assembling a small radio.

"We'll need power," JinJo whispered.

"Well, I can't hold the handlebars," Dr. Havestock showed the old man his minuscule hands, "but perhaps BART here could use her leg to pedal the stationary bike. That should generate enough friction to power the radio."

Less than fifteen minutes later, and the rig was set up. Charlotte, had all manner of diodes and vacuum tubes attached to her teeth. Two alligator clips pinched molars on either side of her jaw. And BART began to pedal.

It started as an itch. A small tingling on Charlotte's gum line. It then increased as BART pedaled faster and faster and generated more energy through Charlotte's braces which would then occasionally arc into her wet gums. Her eyes watered as small flashes of electricity lit up the void inside her mouth.

And then there came the distinct sound of a human voice. A man's, deep and distant, echoing out of Charlotte's mouth. The group smiled. BART laughed. JinJo repositioned one of Charlotte's arms much like one would rabbit ear antennas. With each movement, the man's voice became clearer.

Dr. Havestock reached inside Charlotte's mouth to flip a toggle and instructed JinJo to speak through a makeshift rudimentary microphone.

JinJo spoke, quietly and deliberately. He said who he was, (roughly) where he was, and that he was looking for someone - anyone - out there. When he was done, the small disparate group huddled high above the ruined mass of the oil tanker, sat in silence - waiting.

Charlotte, whose mouth looked like a WWI war zone, and whose gums still ached with the energy pulsing through them, sat quietly.

And from the ether, the radio waves flew through the ghosted air, bounced off the decomposing walls of the *Dairugger*, and sparked wildly inside the metal maze attached to Charlotte's teeth. A voice, loud and curious said, "JinJo, you're coming in loud and clear."

A tear fell down Charlotte's cheek out of hope, happiness, or having thousands of volts of electricity spin through her face.

## The Walk

### *Week Forty Six*

I meet Tilo Gomez at his place of business; 604 feet above the Hudson River. Wearing a blaze orange vest trimmed with a Day-Glo green border, it's easy to spot him behind the gray-blue grating of the bridge tower. Leaning against the metal ties, his eyes are pointed out across the span toward New Jersey. He turns his head slightly when I advance, holding out his hand sideways though remaining vigilant to his duty.

With "security" stamped across the back of his vest, I wonder what he's actually protecting.

"There's ten or so a year. That's the number that actually hit the water. Most weeks we'll get one or two people who stop and look out at the skyline a bit too long. That's when we start the long walk out toward the middle of the bridge." Tilo's shoulders sink in the unmistakable indication that "the walk" is the worst part of his job.

Like all suspension bridges, the George Washington Bridge shifts and sways as its load and the wind currents change. This movement is especially noticeable closer to the ends of the bridge. Tilo doesn't seem to notice it anymore. He's been working security on the bridge for the past three years, before that he'd worked for a private security company guarding children at a public high school in the Bronx. He does not know the exact numbers of "jumpers" he's talked back down over the years, a term I find confusingly used.

"This gig is much better," he says, turning his head toward Inwood and over to the Bronx. "I live up here, so the commute is easier." Tilo was born here, and grew up just off Dyckman Street. His parents came over from the Dominican Republic, a place whose name invokes a large smile from Tilo. He is bilingual, and his Hispanic heritage is reflected in his accent. His voice is quiet, but certain. It could be the ten people a year, but there's a reflection and a purpose to each word he sounds out. They fall off his tongue with a silent prayer affixed to them. As if there's always the possibility that those gentle tones might be the last ones someone may hear.

Tilo laughs when I ask why he doesn't carry a gun. "No, there's no need. You don't pull a gun on a jumper." I realize the stupidity of this question and subconsciously look out and down toward the river. As if to make up for my error, I ask what he'd do if a terrorist wanted to blow up the bridge. He points to his walkie-talkie indicating that would be his first line of defense. "Plus," he says with a knowing smile, "this sucker was built really well. Stuffing a backpack full of explosives would only kill the person wearing it and flake some paint off the side of the bridge."

We walk out on the bridge and I ask him about his family. He tells me about his older brother who is a patent attorney downtown. "He's traveled all over the world. He loves to talk about it, and his feelings and ideas on politics. Mostly I just sit and listen. It's him showing off for himself. Making him feel better about the choices he's made."

"And the choices you've made?" I ask. "How does he feel about you up here on the bridge?"

"He thinks I'm wasting my time. Wasting my life. But he doesn't understand the feeling you get when someone steps back over the guard rail and gives you a hug for saving their life. That's something you can't bottle or get from a tour guide. And no college book can adequately explain that feeling. It's genuine."

We're in the middle of the bridge now, the green waters of the Hudson rush past the submerged rocks of Jeffery's Hook. The River looks both serene and menacing.

"Do you ever get jealous of your brother and his travels?"

Looking back toward the Manhattan tower, Tilo takes a moment and smiles "No, that walk is the longest trip I ever want to make."

## The Heretic's Guide to the Afterlife, Book One

*Week Forty Seven*

Your beliefs brought you here. Or, perhaps, you lack of beliefs. Nevertheless, you are here, and you are welcome. Also, congratulations, you're dead. But really, the most important part isn't that you're here, but how you got here. As they say, it's the journey, not the destination, and fuck it: they were right.

You aren't a dick. Or, more to the point, you weren't a dick. At least not a giant dick. Maybe you accidentally killed a squirrel with your car. Maybe you punched your brother in the stomach - not out of malice - but because the dude fucking deserved it. But when it comes to the global view of things, you were upstanding and maybe perhaps only slightly a dick when necessity demanded it.

You didn't subscribe to some sort of thought control run by a bunch of old white guys in a far off land who seem to think they know what you should believe more than you do. And deeper than that, you aren't basing your life off of the teachings of a book that was written when there were only two items in the periodic table of elements (gold and not gold).

But what you did was good. Literally, you did good. Not "well" in terms of becoming a billionaire by sucking long-dead dinosaurs out of the ocean and converting them into a hyper-flammable substance. No, you brought more good into the world than you took out of it.

And that's a hard thing to accomplish.

Like, really hard. Have you ever been in line at the grocery store and the person in front of you sends their four year-old kid to go find something to add to their check out and it ends up taking the kid five or ten minutes because they don't know fuck all about the difference between diced tomatoes or stewed tomatoes? And all you want to do is stab the customer in the face because they should be punished for their giant mistake of not getting the proper tomatoes when they were in the tomato aisle.

But you didn't. And that makes you good. And when you spread "good," either actively or passively, it has a positive impact on the universe. And when people think about you, either in the present or past tense, they'll think of you as good.

That's fine, you say, but what about those who criticized me for not believing in a higher power? Is there a higher power? Is there anything but a void?

First, let's say there is an all-powerful, all-seeing, and all-knowing, "man upstairs." Do you think they really take comfort in someone/something that let both *Small Wonder* and the 5th *Die Hard* movie be created under their watch? That's just bad judgement.

Second, you're probably noticing now that you aren't about to have lunch with Albert Einstein, or take your dog that was run-over by a car when you were in 3rd grade out for a walk. But what you have done is taken the collective positive energy all these people and creatures brought you, infused it into your life, and spread that positivity and goodwill throughout the world. So they live on, you live on, and the world will live on. You are a higher power just by sharing your love.

Let's say you were a dick. Let's say you told people how to live their lives based on your ideas, or you shunned people because they believed different things than you. Guess what, you were a dick then, you're a dick now, and people are going to remember you for being a dick. Adolf Hitler was a supreme dick, and no one these days is saying how well he treated his dogs or how great his casserole was - unless the person saying it is also a dick.

Positivity and negativity are virulent, but on the tipping scales of infinite justice, it was positivity that won out in your life.

So, where do we go from here?

Close your eyes and it all goes away. Or stay wide-eyed and watch the light of the stars blink out one by one.

## Blink

*Week Forty Eight*

Heather Feather's favorite time of day was when the sun set and the sky turned from orange, to pink, to purple. As a firefly, it was the best time for her family to leave their home and blink and dance above the grass.

Each firefly family had their own way of blinking. The Drift family went *Blinky Blink Blinky Blink,* and the Woodspot family went *BaBlink BaBlink BaBlink*. But Heather Feather's family went *Blink Blink BaBlink.*

"Dad," Heather Feather asked, "Why do we always go *Blink Blink BaBlink*?"

"That's how we can find each other in the darkness," Heather Feather's father responded as he walked to their front door.

"Oh," thought Heather Feather, still not convinced.

She looked out over the small rolling hills and saw thousands of firefly lights turning on and off across the landscape.

"Ready! Steady! Go!!" yelled Heather Feather's Father as the Feather family jumped out of their home and flew into the yard.

Heather Feather watched as her father, her mother, and her little brother danced and blinked with all the other families in their neighborhood, but only her family went *Blink Blink BaBlink.*

She decided then and there that she was going to blink however she wanted to. And darting over the grass, Heather Feather went *Blinky BaBlink*

*Blink Blink*. She flew through flowers, past a grove of mushrooms, and over a hedge shaped like a duck. All the while, blinking the way she wanted to blink.

*Blink Blink Blinky BaBlinky Blink Blinky Blink.*

Heather Feather picked up speed, skimming over the waters of the small brook that trickled through the woods, and hopped up rocks piled near the shore. With each blink, she felt more powerful and independent, and she imagined a trail of light following close behind her.

Suddenly, she found herself deep in the forest, away from her neighborhood and her family.

She blinked once. Then twice. But no one blinked in return.

She tried to retrace her flight, but only felt herself growing more and more lost.

In all her blinking, she'd forgotten how she'd gotten here, and she could feel the dark and towering trees closing in around her. A cold northern wind began to blow. Heather Feather was all alone. She landed on a fallen log and, feeling that all hope was lost, began to cry.

Heather Feather tried blinking again - a dim single blink - but again, got no response. Finally, in a last attempt, she went *Blink Blink BaBlink.*

Somewhere, deep outside the forest, she saw three tiny lights go *Blink Blink BaBlink.*

With a start, she began to fly toward the lights, and the lights began flying toward her. Closer now, she could see that it was her father, mother, and brother racing quickly to her.

Heather Feather flew right into her mother's arms, then kissed her little brother on the cheek, and finally gave her father the biggest hug she could possibly muster.

"I'm sorry, Dad" Heather Feather said with tears in her eyes, "I should never have tried to blink differently."

Heather Feather's Father hugged her tightly and said, "Oh Heather Feather, you can blink however you want to blink. We only blink the way we do because it reminds us that we're a family. We want you to blink in whatever way makes you happy. And if you ever need us, just go *Blink Blink BaBlink*, and the entire family will be there to help."

"Thanks Dad," she said and pressed her face deeper into her father's arm and used his shirt to wipe away her tears.

The entire family flew back to their home together, happy that they'd found Heather Feather safe.

And when she'd finally gotten cozy in her bed and just before shutting her eyes to fall asleep, Heather Feather went *Blink Blink BaBlink* and smiled.

## The Mad Bomber

*Week Forty Nine*

The photos were pinned to the large board hanging in Henley Whippenscoot's office - creating a mosaic of hyper-saturated dresses, glinting jewels, and smiles that had been perfected by either years of walking red carpets or by the hands and knives of the best plastic surgeons in Beverly Hills.

Henley fell back into her chair with a breath, and took in the collection. Each photo had been culled down from the nearly 3,000 taken at the annual *Marks Museum Fundraiser for Underprivileged Cavalier King Charles Spaniel Puppies.* A showcase for the Hollywood, Washington, and, lately, North Dakotan elite, the gala was the place to see and be seen, and, of course, raise a few thousand dollars for the poor - both literally and figuratively - show dogs.

As fashion editor for *Touched,* the definitive magazine for bored housewives who wanted to stare at millionaires' cleavage while also learning 101 ways to please their men, Henley Whippenscoot needed to select *the* photo to grace the cover of the December issue. She let her eyes blur and glazed over the patches of Ibizan chartreuse, broken fender platinum grey, and *Fiji Water* label cyan.

Almost instinctively, she grabbed one image of Madison Light, recent star of the romantic comedy, *Why Not? Let's Have a Baby!,* and Jasmine Portnoy who never did anything of note, other than having been recorded in the midst of various sexual acts and sending those recordings to various news outlets.

Henley placed both photos on her desk and took in every detail. Her red sharpie would indicate where retouching would need to go back and remove birthmarks, underboobs, overboobs, wispy hairs, too many minorities, and, of course, unsightly wrinkles. Casually, she circled a man just beyond Jasmine's right buttcheek giving the tell-tale "Home Alone" two-hands on the cheeks surprised look.

Moving on to Madison, she circled Madison's shoulder freckles, a strange shadow on her upper lip, and an item in her purse that was, without a doubt, cocaine. Then she noticed him, the same man giving the Home Alone look. Same guy. Same expression. Henley circled him again, and muttered, "photobombing son of a bitch" under her breath.

She placed both photos into an envelope and handed them to her assistant to send to retouching. She went back to the wall and began removing the other photos from the board, and that's when she noticed him: the same guy. In every single photo. Making the same exact face. She laughed at the man's simple effort. But then she saw that this was no small feat.

The man moved. He was in different locations. He had strategically placed himself behind these celebrities just as they had their photos taken. And because Henley had four different photographers working the event in four different areas, this man was incredibly dedicated to, dare she say it, his *craft.*

She circled another photo of the man, this time as he stood shocked and barely visible behind the gargantuan and ostentatious violet peacock hat worn by Desdemona Beatrice, a long faded actress whose decades of cigarette smoking made the lines around her lips look like the indentations on the bottom of baccarat tumblers.

Henley squinted to get a better look at this strange person who put the effort into such a random task and questioned out loud, "Who are you, man?"

---

"Ha! Look at this one," Sam said, turning the iPad around so his wife, Karen, could see the digital photo more clearly, "Mark is photobombing us."

"That's too bad," Karen said, shrugging her nose, "It's probably the best one we have."

Sam looked closer at the picture, scrutinized it, used his hands to figure out a way to crop Mark out. Finally, he laughed, "Let's use it. It'll be funny, and I'm sure Mark would get a kick out of it."

"Fine. But I get to pick the photo for next year's holiday card."

---

Across town, Herb Fieldspar could just make out the illuminated spire of the Meridian Publishing building, the same multinational media company that published *Touched*. He wondered what Henley was going to choose for the cover of her December issue. He'd settled on an Eastern European model posing in a barely there swimsuit amidst the ruined walls overlooking the Bay of Kotor in Montenegro. If anything said merry and festive for the holiday season, this image was it, and it was destined for the cover of *Drop In* magazine's Christmas issue.

Herb, being old-school, held his magnifying glass over the picture in an attempt to find any flaws. He made a few notes about pumping up the lighting in certain areas, removing wayward trees, and having the model's eyes changed from brown to blue.

Giving the photo a final pass, he noticed him. Small. Barely noticeable with the naked eye. A man holding his hands to his face like that Culkin kid in that one movie. Herb grabbed other photos from the same shoot and recognized the guy time and time again.

Jesus this guy was persistent.

The photo, along with a request to airbrush out the man, was sent to retouching. Herb sat at his desk and called Henley. It was common courtesy for the two rivals to call each other once they'd decided on who would be gracing each issue's cover. As main rivals, they never wanted to feature the same person. And, if Herb were being honest, he liked hearing Henley's voice.

"It's between Madison Light and Jasmine Portnoy," said Henley into the phone. "We'll probably go with Madison because she said she'd attend our *Free Alaska* charity event in February."

"Great choice," Herb said. "Yeah, we've got some up and coming girl from Hungary or Lithuania or some shit on ours."

"Oh, so get this. I've got some asshole in the back of every single one of my photos making the *Home Alone* face."

"What?"

"Seriously. Every single photo has this guy making the same photo. It's unbelievable."

"Uh… are you serious? Because I had the same exact problem."

"Herb, don't fuck with me."

"I'm not fucking with you, Henley. Hold on, I'll text you an image."

Herb snapped the image quickly with his phone and sent it to Henley.

"Herb. This is the same goddamn guy."

"No way. Not possible."

"I'm sure of it. Same guy. Same expression."

"Are you saying that this guy just goes around town - hell, the world, and photobombs?"

"Unless you're playing a trick on me."

"Henley, I promise on all that is holy, I'm not playing a trick on you."

Henley snapped the work-in-progress photo for *Touched* and sent it to Herb.

"What? The? Hell?"

---

The Butcher's holiday card sat on top of catalogs, bills, and books of coupons promising end of the year savings. Mark grabbed the stack of mail from the mailbox and threw it into the passenger seat of his car. He noticed the Butcher's home address and quickly pulled the car over to see if he'd made the cut.

There, behind the smiling faces of the Butcher clan and a note about wishes and holidays, was Mark's unmistakable shocked expression. Mark smiled an almost evil smirk - one filled with happiness, deceitfulness, and knowing.

---

A basketball star going for a game-winning slam dunk in the finals? There was the guy with the shocked expression sitting in the seats.

A guitarist mid-solo and illuminated by a point of stage light, and yet somehow the guy with the shocked expression made his way into the frame.

A magazine photo accompanying an article about the dangers of slip fishing, and on a boat hundreds of miles off of shore stood the guy with the shocked expression.

No one knew who he was. But a small team of both amateur and professional detectives, AI-fueled programmers, and devoted journalists were determined to find out.

---

The following year, the Butchers asked Mark to be in their holiday card again. Same guy. Same expression. Mark turned them down.

Few people recognize their talents. Fewer still recognize the importance of not exploiting their talents. Mark was no sellout. He realized what he had, and he'd decided early on that each photobomb would be special. Unforced. Crafted. Perfect.

---

As the limos carrying the A-listers lined up outside the theater, the technicians went to work. Facial recognition software was humming from a server-truck just offsite. Panoramic cameras saw every zit, scar, and facial hair of every single person in a three-block radius. Every photographer at the event had their cameras outfitted with software that would recognize him instantly in their view finder. If the Mad Bomber were to strike, they'd know before he ever set foot on the property.

The Mad Bomber appeared in so many photos that they knew exactly what he looked like. A team of psychologists assembled a dossier on his personality. And everyone agreed, were he to strike, the *Narcissus Awards* were the absolute ideal place to do his dirty work.

None of the stars were aware of the threat. No security teams were alerted. The increase in surveillance was claimed to be a by-the-book terrorist threat. The analysts feared if the Mad Bomber caught wind of the increase in security, he'd back out of his plan.

The team watched the monitors diligently. Fingers tapped on desks. Other fingers had their nails gnawed by nervous magazine editors. This sting operation was better funded, and more detailed than the night they killed Bin Laden.

"Nothing," said Gragson hunched toward his monitor. "No hits."

"He's here. I can feel it," replied Wilkes-Barre grabbing Gragson's joystick and moving the security camera around the property. To herself, almost inaudibly, she said, "Where the hell are you?"

"I think I've got something!" One of the technicians whose name Wilkes-Barre had purposefully forgotten raised his hand. Wilkes-Barre rushed to him.

"Show me."

"I got a hit. At least I thought I did," he said nervously, feeling Wilkes-Barre's breath on the back of his neck.

"How sure are you?"

"80... 90 percent," he stuttered nervously.

"Out!" Wilkes-Barre moved his seat back and launched him out of the chair. She quickly scanned the monitor's image, squinting into each shadow and corner. But she saw nothing. She picked up her radio, "Blue 5, can you do a sweep of area x-2 to area y-9? We need confirmation on a potential spotting."

"Roger," came the static-filled voice of Blue 5.

Wilkes-Barre changed her view to Blue 5's body cam, and followed as he ran through the area, scanning in a *Z* formation.

"Status, Blue 5?"

"Uh… that's a negative. I've got nothing."

"He's there. He's somewhere!" Wilkes-Barre was at her wit's end.

Half a mile away, celebrities were smiling as they leisurely walked the red carpet. Dresses were picked apart. Comments were made under breaths. And a man stood behind all of them with his hands pressed to his cheeks and his mouth agape.

And no one saw.

---

Mark's face was on every major newspaper. He was in the background for entertainment television packages. He even managed to look up with the same expression just as a blimp was broadcasting overhead.

The public caught wind of Mark's endeavors and quickly turned him into a folk hero. Websites were set up in an attempt to identify him. Others claimed he was their brother, their cousin, their boyfriend. But despite all of this, no one knew who he was, and the Mad Bomber lived on.

---

While families of other eleven year old kids took them to Florida or California, Mark's family took him to Oslo, Norway. Walking around the city's harbor, they hopped from landmark to landmark, museum to museum. Bored, and tired, Mark purposefully dragged his feet as his family slowly walked the queue to enter the National Gallery. Once inside, he saw hundreds of paintings of long dead people, unrealistic landscapes, and out-of-proportion statues that left him seething with jealousy about his best friend, whose parents had taken him to the just-opened *Walt Disney World*.

"This next painting is very special," Mark's mom said pointing toward a swirl of colors with a skeletal-like man screaming in the foreground. "It was painted by a man named Edvard Munch."

Mark's eyes slowly lifted through the veil of malaise and half-heartedly looked at the painting. He felt his pupils widen and a rush of heat ran through his body and electrified the ends of his hair.

This painting was something else. He walked up to *The Scream* and attempted to take in every single part of it. The twisted body and sky. The deep colors of sunset. And the pained expression of man. He wanted nothing more than to be this man, releasing his anger, his boredom, and his confusion. And deep in the back of his mind, a fire was lit. Small but not insignificant. He determined right then and there that, throughout his life, he'd bring the scream to people whose lives had been leveled with boredom. He'd provide an outlet, some joy, and a way of reaching through the madness to allow people to laugh at the absurd.

He became the Mad Bomber.

## The Great Beyond

*Week Fifty*

She wanted something simple.

"You're not going to need it long," she'd say, looking through what one might consider to be the most melancholy catalog ever devised.

It's a strange thing to sit there next to your dying girlfriend, and picking out which urn she'd like most.

"Just pick the one you like most," she said, closing the catalog. "Or go cheap. Honestly, I don't care and I won't be there to enjoy it. But promise me you'll turn it into something awesome, like a vase or a place to store your car keys."

We spent our last few days together imagining what our timeline looked like if it unspooled indefinitely. Where we'd get married. What we'd name our kids. What color we'd paint our house. And as I held her and heard the furnace of her lungs expel what would be one of the last thousand or so breaths they'd take, she said she wished we could ice skate on a frozen pond in the moonlight. Just once.

I didn't ice skate. She didn't ice skate. And, it was summer.

"We'd float below the stars," she said, her voice tiny and delicate, "making parallel twists and dancing to the sound of nothing." She exhaled again in resignation, "It would all be so wonderful."

---

I stood on the edge of the lake holding what remained of her in a minimalist yet tasteful box. Through moistened eyes, I opened the lid and spilled her into the water which created a fitting reverse mushroom cloud of smoke that drifted with the wind.

I watched her fade away in the bleach of the summer sun, then walked home in my cheap suit to work on the rest of my life.

---

*Hey,*
*So, I'm dead, huh?*

Of course she left me a note. She probably had one of the nurses mail it for her. It felt odd to hold a piece of paper that she'd held only a week ago. I lifted it to my nose to see if it smelled like her.

*I'm sorry I won't be around to name our children after characters from the Lord of the Rings. Quick side note here: whomever you do end up with, please don't make her name your kids after characters from the Lord of the Rings. Naming a kid 'Strider' is child abuse.*

She continued through all the normal things, such as thanking me for helping her, reminding me how much she loved me, and asking me to feed the cat. But it was the last couple of lines that stood out.

*And I have a task for you. Go out. Talk to people. Engage. You've never been Mr. Social, but now is the time. You'll never find someone who loves you as much as I do by sitting at home. Go to restaurants. Travel. Experience the world. But more than anything, talk to people.*

I hadn't had many friends since grade school, and those I did grew distant once she got sick. I hated social situations, and would rather stay at home with movies, video games, or my books. But how could I not honor my dead girlfriend's final wish?

Even in her death, I still spun upon her finger.

---

The photo's edges had frayed. The colors muted. And yet I could still hear her laugh echoing through infinity as she felt the wind turn her hair into a cone of drift and chaos. I placed the photo gingerly into my coat pocket and looked at the back of my coffee cup and into the empty chair beyond the wooden cliff of the cafe table.

I began slowly, simply smiling at people as they passed my table. The toothless lips pressed tight expression one would reserve for passing a co-worker in the office cafeteria. I got many in return, but the closest I got to legitimate conversation was when a young father asked to take the empty chair reserved for my dead girlfriend to let his daughter sit down.

The next day, I sat in the same chair at the same table in the same cafe. Granted, this wasn't the most proactive way of engaging in conversations with strangers, but I needed to take baby steps. The sun shrunk shadows and then drew them long as I sat quietly sipping various coffees, waters, and ate a variety of cafe foods. I sketched ideas in a notepad, and assigned names and personalities to the birds that ate crumbs off the sidewalk.

And as the lights blinked on in the windows of the buildings across the street, each new illuminated square of sidewalk drove home the point that I was failing to live up to the one wish my girlfriend had requested of me. I left without a word and spent the night connecting dots on my ceiling to distract me from my failures.

---

Silence has a way of drawing people in. We are a vocal species, and the lack of talk will drive others to think something is wrong. Such was the case as I sat in the cafe on the third day.

"You alright man?" he asked with a mix of concern and amicable uplift, "Noticed you've been sitting here just looking off into space."

"Yeah! I'm great," I lied. "Just lost in thought."

"Alright man. We'll I hope they're good thoughts."

"They are," another lie. What would *she* do? And then, the impossible, "How are YOU doing?"

"I'm good," he said, sitting down across from me. "I mean, 'good' is relative, right? My shoulder hasn't been the same since I fell snowboarding last winter. My girl thinks I'm not passionate enough. And I'm pretty sure my boss is embezzling funds from our firm. But I'm not homeless. So I'm good."

"Right on," I said having never actually used the term 'right on' before. Ever. "Out of those, which is the most concerning?"

"Damn. I guess the passionate thing. She's awesome and I'm completely undeserving of her. But that's probably the easiest to fix. The shoulder is really just me procrastinating going to the doctor, and my boss is an asshole who deserves whatever is coming to him."

In the background, a server called out an order that I didn't hear.

"Shit, that's me. Good talking to you man." and he got up, grabbed his coffee, and walked out the door.

I'd engaged. I asked questions. I learned something about someone else. I gravitated.

---

"I like your shoes," I said, not knowing if I was supposed to like her shoes.

"Thanks," she said with a warm smile. "They're [insert some fancy brand I've never heard of here] and they hurt like hell."

"You wanna take a seat?"

"Thanks, but I'm already late for a meeting. Next time?"

She walked to the door and stopped before opening it. "I like your shoes, too," she said before walking into the sunlight.

---

That night, I took a dramatic step. I took a piece of paper, folded it in half lengthwise, and wrote "Free to Listen" on either side. The next day, I placed it in front of me.

And they showed up.

All of them.

The ones who wanted to talk. The ones who wanted to have someone listen. The ones who had a world to unleash, and those who needed to know that they were heard.

One woman talked about the prettiest rose she'd ever seen that just happened to be growing a few blocks away. A man spoke about being disconnected from his son. A little girl talked - at great length - about her favorite stuffed sheep. One couple asked me if I thought they should move in together. Another woman asked me to watch her puppy while she ordered.

I left that day feeling energized, like my body were filled with humanity in a way that I hadn't felt since she died.

I'd bring the sign with me again tomorrow.

---

"Well, what do you think?" she asked, her eyes tracing the wood grain of the table top.

"I think you should call him. I know a thing or two about true love, and if you really think that's what you guys have, don't let distance get in the way."

I'd been actively talking to people for more than two weeks, each day more and more people lined up to talk. I'd heard all manner of stories, and almost all of them came down to one simple thing: needing a human connection.

"You're right. I'm sure I can get a job out in Denver. Sometimes you need to jump without looking, right?" she said, now looking directly at me hoping for some facial reassurance.

"If it's true love, it's not really like jumping at all."

"This has been awesome. Thank you so much. So what about you? What's your deal?"

"I don't have a deal."

"My friend, anyone who solicits conversations with strangers has a deal. What's yours?"

"Ha," I looked away trying to find the right words. "Well, it comes down to loneliness, I guess."

"All this because you wanted to talk to someone? Isn't that what internet chat rooms are for?"

"Well, there's more to it than that."

"Go on," and with her words I felt my jaw tighten and my voice became weak.

"My girlfriend died a month ago, and one of her last wishes was that I be more social," she instinctively reached across the table and held my hand. I could feel my eyes grow heavy.

"Well, it seems like you're doing a good job of being social."

"So it would seem. It hasn't been easy," now I was being sheepish.

"You've been coming here for the past month since she died and just hoping to talk to anyone? I'm sure you've heard all sorts of stories. But what's your story? Tell me about her."

Cue the floodgates. I told her everything. How we met. How she liked her waffles. What happened when she got sick, and what happened afterward. She never interrupted. She didn't ask questions. She just listened. And in that moment, it felt like all this pain and sadness that I was holding inside just escaped and melted into the ether.

When I was done, she smiled, thanked me, and walked away without saying another word.

---

I slept more deeply and more completely than I had in weeks. It was the first time since she died that I dreamed. And when I woke up in the morning, I saw my "Free to Listen" sign sitting on our kitchen table. I immediately tossed it in the trash and grabbed another piece of paper which I folded lengthwise. On either side, I wrote, "Free to Talk."

## Please Can You Stop the Noise I'm Trying to Get Some Rest

*Week Fifty One*

"You'll find this first painting unpleasant," the tour guide, who'd given his one syllable name to the group of which all but two had promptly forgotten it, said walking backwards and stopping before a crushed velvet rope in faded white. And, as he was in the process of assigning feelings to people without much consideration for their personalities, many took it upon themselves to determine the pleasant or unpleasantness of the painting for themselves. Some turned up their noses. Others squinted with downturned mouths. Others shrugged and continued on as if they hadn't bore witness to what art critics had deemed was the artist's "most horrid piece."

The info card that sat firmly next to every other piece of art in the museum was conspicuously missing from the painting. When the artwork arrived at the museum, it was without a title, an artist, or a history. It sat in storage for years until a new curator chose it to appear in an exhibit titled *Rogues Gallery* in which all the pieces were by unknown authorship. This particular painting with its morbid depiction caused quite a stir that the curator, deciding to drum up some press, kept it hung after the exhibit was over.

As the group continued on under the disciplined lead of Tom, or Bob, or Pete, or Greg, one girl stood behind unaware that the cluster of tourists had moved on. She smiled at the painting and the painting smiled back.

## The Stories

### *Week Fifty Two*

The old man watched the sand castles, saturated by the incoming tide, crumble into softened heaps. His grandchildren danced on the beach, and ran from the waves as they broke on the sand. He closed his notebook, using his pen to hold his place and took in the scene. His youngest granddaughter came running up to him with a shell in her hand.

"Grandpa! Look what I found!" she said, thrusting it in his face, "Isn't it beautiful?

"It is," he answered, "It truly is."

Her attention immediately shifted from the shell to her grandfather's notebook.

"Grandpa, what is that?"

"It's my notebook."

"What do you do with it?"

"I write stories, notes, and other ideas in it."

"Why?"

The old man laughed. He'd never thought about why. In fact, he feared, if he stopped and thought about why he did it, he'd see its futility and never pick up the pen again. Smiling and taking a deep breath to gather his thoughts, he looked down at his granddaughter and said, "Because, when I was your age, I'd spend my days staring out the window. I'd imagine myself on far off adventures, or watch fictional dogfights happening in the skies over my school yard. To help quiet my mind before I went to sleep each night, I'd craft intricate stories about my friends and family, and picture us looking for lost pirate gold, or racing cars through the countryside."

"Oh," she said, "But why do you write them down?"

"Well, I suppose it's selfish. I hope that other people would like to read these stories and enjoy them. Maybe it'll inspire them to write stories of their own," he paused and collected his thoughts again. "But perhaps more than anything, it's a way to make these dreams tangible. To make them real. You see, someday I'm going to forget what it felt like to watch you and your siblings play on the beach. I'll forget what it's like to have the salt water dry in crystals on my arm. And, I'll forget this moment of us sitting here talking. But if I can write these moments and thoughts down, and describe them in a way the gives them life, well then they live forever."

"Have you ever written about me?"

"Of course," he said, tucking a long strand of hair behind her ear. "You're in every one of my stories. You might be a tree, or a cloud. Maybe you'll be a thought or a word. And sometimes, you're front and center. You may not look like yourself, but you're always there."

The girl looked back at her grandfather's notebook. "Can I write a story in your notebook?"

"Absolutely. I'd love it," he said, opening the book to a blank page.

"What should I write about?" she asked.

Handing his granddaughter his pen he said, "Anything you want."

# Acknowledgements

I'd like to thank my wife, Lindsey, and daughter, Malin, for all that they do for me, not the least of which is giving me the time and patience to write. Your support made this all worthwhile. I'm especially grateful to friend and pseudo-cousin, Sam Butcher, for his incredible feedback, encouragement, and story ideas. Thanks also to Peter Gagnon for his motivation and helping me realize my need to create something.

I'd be remiss not to mention my small cadre of "writer friends" who've, one way or another, helped push me forward. They include: Sarah Huntington, Tod Williams, Ernest White II, Elisabeth Wild, Steve Coulson, Kelly Turner, Anna David, Eric Paschal Johnson, Neil Turitz, Bjorn Turmann, Phil Rossi, and Johnny Wright.

Finally, a deep debt of sincere gratitude and love to my parents, Peter and Dana, and my brother, Eric.

## About the Author

Adam Drake lives in Connecticut with his wife, daughter, and a cat who controls the weather.

www.ingramcontent.com/pod-product-compliance
Lightning Source LLC
Chambersburg PA
CBHW030816310726
48980CB00006B/522/J

* 9 7 8 0 5 7 8 4 4 2 9 0 7 *